The Stranger from Abilene

**Center Point
Large Print**

Also by Joseph A. West
and available from Center Point Large Print:

Burning Range

**This Large Print Book carries the
Seal of Approval of N.A.V.H.**

Ralph Compton

The Stranger
from Abilene

A Ralph Compton Novel
by Joseph A. West

CENTER POINT LARGE PRINT
THORNDIKE, MAINE

This Center Point Large Print edition
is published in the year 2012 by arrangement with
NAL Signet, a member of Penguin Group (USA) Inc.

The text of this Large Print edition is unabridged.
In other aspects, this book may vary
from the original edition.
Printed in the United States of America
on permanent paper.
Set in 16-point Times New Roman type.

ISBN: 978-1-61173-334-1

Library of Congress Cataloging-in-Publication Data

West, Joseph A.
The stranger from Abilene : a Ralph Compton novel / by Joseph A.
West. — Center Point large print ed.
p. cm.
ISBN 978-1-61173-334-1 (lib. bdg. : alk. paper)
1. Large type books. I. Compton, Ralph. II. Title.
PS3573.E8224S77 2012
813'.54—dc23
                                                    2011052428

THE IMMORTAL COWBOY

This is respectfully dedicated to the "American Cowboy." His was the saga sparked by the turmoil that followed the Civil War, and the passing of more than a century has by no means diminished the flame.

True, the old days and the old ways are but treasured memories, and the old trails have grown dim with the ravages of time, but the spirit of the cowboy lives on.

In my travels—to Texas, Oklahoma, Kansas, Nebraska, Colorado, Wyoming, New Mexico, and Arizona—I always find something that reminds me of the Old West. While I am walking these plains and mountains for the first time, there is this feeling that a part of me is eternal, that I have known these old trails before. I believe it is the undying spirit of the frontier calling me, through the mind's eye, to step back into time. What is the appeal of the Old West of the American frontier?

It has been epitomized by some as the dark and bloody period in American history. Its heroes—Crockett, Bowie, Hickok, Earp—have been reviled and criticized. Yet the Old West lives on, larger than life.

It has become a symbol of freedom, when there was always another mountain to climb and another river to cross; when a dispute between two men was settled not with expensive lawyers, but with fists, knives, or guns. Barbaric? Maybe. But some things never change. When the cowboy rode into the pages of American history, he left behind a legacy that lives within the hearts of us all.

—*Ralph Compton*

Chapter 1

It was midnight when the man from Abilene came to the ferry.

He could have been there earlier, but had taken his time along the trail, in no hurry to kill the man he hunted.

A steel triangle hung from a rope, suspended from the low branch of a cottonwood that stood by the riverbank. Tied to the triangle was a length of scrap iron.

The man—tall, lanky, the weight of forty hard years hanging heavy on him—groaned as he swung stiffly out of the saddle. He led his pony to the river and let it drink.

A bloodstained moon had impaled itself on a pine on the opposite bank, and the night was still, the silence as fragile as glass.

Only the misted river talked, an ebb and flow of whispers as it washed back and forth over a sand and shingle bank.

The night was cool, the stars frosted.

Once the buckskin had drunk its fill, the man led it back to the triangle.

He grabbed the chunk of iron and clattered and clanged the triangle awake, its racketing clamor ringing through the splintering night.

The man smiled and twenty years fled from his weathered face. He dropped the iron, mightily pleased by his act of acoustic vandalism.

A couple of echoing minutes passed, and a couple more.

He heard a splash from the far bank; then a man's voice, cranky, rusted with age, reached out through the darkness to him.

"Hell, did you have to wake the whole damned county?"

The man from Abilene grinned and made no answer.

But the ferryman, invisible in the darkness, wouldn't let it go.

"Alarming good Christian folks like that. 'Tain't right and 'tain't proper."

The man, still grinning, took hold of the iron again and banged it lightly against the triangle, once, twice, three times.

"And that ain't funny," the ferryman yelled.

The ferry, a large raft with a pole rail on two sides, emerged from the mist like a creature rising from a primordial swamp. Its algae-covered logs ground over shingle and shuddered to a stop.

"Howdy," the man from Abilene said, raising a hand in greeting.

The ferryman dropped the rope he'd been hauling. Even in the darkness he looked sour.

"You the ranny making all the noise?" he said.

"Sorry I had to wake you," the man said.

"Hell, you could've camped out tonight and rang the bell in the morning when folks are awake."

The man nodded. "Maybe so, but I'm mighty tired of my own cooking and spreading my blankets on rocks and scorpions."

The ferryman was old and he'd lived that long by being careful around tall night riders with eyes that saw clean through a man to what lay within, good or bad.

Like this one.

"You won't find no vittles or soft bed around here," he said.

"There's a town just three miles west of the river," the tall man said. "Or so I was told."

The ferryman nodded. "You was told right. But Bighorn Point is a quiet place. God-fearing people living there, and everything closes at eleven, even on Friday nights."

He gave the tall man a sideways look. "There ain't no whores in Bighorn Point."

The man from Abilene smiled and flicked the triangle with the nail of his middle finger. As the steel tinged he said, "Right now all I want is food and a bed. I guess I'll just have to wake up some o' them God-fearing folks."

The old man shook his head. "Well, just don't let Marshal Kelly catch you doing that. He'll call it disturbin' the peace an' throw you in the hoosegow quicker'n scat."

Suddenly the tall man was wary. "Would that be Nook Kelly, out of the Sabine River country down Texas way?"

"It be. You know him?"

The tall man shook his head. "Heard of him, is all."

"Nook Kelly has killed fifty men."

"So they say."

"Do you believe it?"

"I'd need to hear it from Kelly himself. People believe what they want to believe."

The man showed the ferryman an empty face, but inwardly he was worried. Having a named gunslinger like Kelly as the law in Bighorn Point was a complication he didn't need.

Ferrymen were spawned by the same demon as trail cooks, and curiosity was one of the many traits they shared.

Interest glowed in the old man's eyes, like a cat studying a rat. "Here, you ain't thinking of robbing the Bighorn Point Mercantile Bank, are ye?"

The tall man smiled. "Now, why would I do a fool thing like that?"

The ferryman looked sly. "Mister, you're a hard case. Seen that right off. You're dressed like a cattleman, but you've seen better days. Except for the new John B. on your head, your duds are so worn I wouldn't give you two bits for the lot, including the boots."

The old man grinned. "Maybe that's why you planned on doing a fool thing like trying to rob the Mercantile."

Getting no answer, he said, "But Nook Kelly would kill you. You know that now."

The tall man said, "Talking yourself out of a fare, ain't you?"

"No. You'll cross the Rubicon because you're headed to Bighorn Point for another reason."

The oldster's historical reference didn't surprise the man from Abilene. Back in the day, this old coot could have been anything.

"You're right," he said. "I'm going to Bighorn Point to kill a man."

"Anybody I know?"

"Maybe. But I don't know the man myself. Hell, I don't even know his name."

"You mean you aim to kill a man, but you don't know who he is?"

"That's how she shakes out, I reckon."

"Mister, he must have done something powerful bad."

The tall man nodded. "Bad enough."

"How you plan on finding him?"

The tall man smiled. "He'll look like he needs killing."

Chapter 2

Bighorn Point was a cow town like any other. Its single street was lined on both sides with false-fronted clapboard buildings that held the place together like bookends.

11

A rising wind kicked up veils of dust from the street, and hanging signs outside the stores screeched on rusty chains.

Oil reflector lamps marched in lockstep along the boardwalks, but those, like every other light in town, were dowsed.

The man from Abilene walked the buckskin to the end of the street, where a church blocked his way, its tall and lonesome steeple like an upraised hand, defying him to ride farther.

The church was too big and ostentatious for the town, a high-maintenance pile as out of place as a rich Boston belle at a prairie hootenanny.

It was a powerful symbol of the church militant, proclaiming to all and sundry, "This is a God-fearing town and we aim to keep it that way."

The tall man lit a cigarette, then slowly walked his horse back the way he'd come.

He saw only one saloon, the Windy Hall, squeezed meekly between a hardware store and a ladies' dress and hat shop.

The place was as quiet as the dark end of a tomb.

Again the man drew rein. The end of the cigarette in his mouth glowed like a firefly in the gloom.

Across the street to his left was a fair-sized hotel, but that too was locked and shuttered, its guests apparently enjoying the sleep of the just.

"Try the livery stable, or pass on through."

The male voice came from behind him, and the

man from Abilene stiffened. He was irritated that he'd allowed someone to walk up on him like that.

Without turning, he said, "You must be the only person in town who's still awake."

"I don't sleep much. Get to my age and bad memories crowd in on a man, keep him from his rest."

There had been humor in the voice and a hint of it lingered in the blue eyes that looked up at the man on the horse.

"We don't get many night riders through Bighorn Point."

"Figured that out my own self."

"Name's Nook Kelly. I'm the town marshal."

"Figured that as well."

"You heard of me?"

"Yeah. Some good, some bad."

Kelly accepted that and said, "You're not an outlaw. You look too steady at a man."

"I'm a rancher. From up Abilene way."

"You got a name?"

"The one my ma and pa gave me."

"You care to share it?"

"Name's Micajah."

"It's a mouthful, but only half a handle."

"Clayton."

"Does anybody call you Micajah without getting shot?"

"My friends call me Cage."

13

"Well, I ain't your friend, so I'll call you Mr. Clayton."

"Suit yourself."

Kelly was short, reed thin, two .450-caliber British Bulldog revolvers hanging from shoulder holsters on each side of his narrow chest.

He could have been any age, though if you studied the lines on his face closely, forty would have been as good a guess as any.

The ferryman had said that Kelly had killed fifty men. That was an exaggeration. He'd killed thirteen in fair fights, seven more in concert with other lawmen.

He was exactly what he seemed to Cage Clayton, A cool, professional killer who had mastered his craft, the way of the revolver, and the understanding of the manner and habit of violent men.

"Why are you in Bighorn Point, Mr. Clayton?"

The man from Abilene hesitated. His showdown with Nook Kelly had come earlier than he'd planned.

But the marshal had a right to know. Besides, he'd spread the word—if he didn't cut loose with his guns right away.

"I'm here to kill a man."

A career gunman is trained not to show his emotions, and Kelly was no exception. He absorbed Clayton's words like a sponge, his face unchanging.

But he was ready. Men like Kelly always were.

"Is it me?"

"I don't know," Clayton said. "But I reckon you're a tad too young."

"What's the name of the man you plan to kill?"

"I don't have that information."

"Met him before, back along the trail?"

Clayton shook his head—then realized it was the kind of momentary lapse that could get him killed around a man like Kelly.

You idiot, Cage! Never take your eyes off his gun hand!

Aloud, he said, "No. I don't know the man."

Kelly smiled, about as warm as a snake grin. "Then how will you know who to kill?"

"Because he'll try to kill me first. Then I'll have him pegged as the one."

Chapter 3

Nook Kelly took a step back, and for a moment Clayton thought he was going to draw. He recalled the lawman's reputation and figured he was a dead man.

But the marshal raised a hand, index finger extended, aimed at Clayton's face, and then dropped it until it pointed at the ground. "Step down. Walk with me."

Clayton swung out of the saddle. Now that he stood beside Kelly, he was struck by how small the man was, his own rangy six feet dwarfing him.

"Walk where?" he asked.

"To the livery. I'll see you bedded down for the night."

"I'm hungry."

"Benny Hinton always has coffee and stew on the stove. He's an old range cook, and habit dies hard."

Clayton hesitated. "I reckoned you'd draw down on me for sure."

"I'm studying on it," Kelly said. "Give me time."

Hinton was a sour, stringy old man, badly stove up, with a slow, stiff-kneed walk.

"Benny, can you take care of this feller's horse, then bed him down and fix him up with grub?" the marshal said.

"Cost him."

"You got money, Mr. Clayton?"

Clayton looked at Hinton. "How much?"

"One dollar for man and hoss, two bits extry fer the grub."

"Your prices run dear."

"Take it or leave it."

"Pay the man, Mr. Clayton," Kelly said. "Or go hungry."

Clayton paid with ill grace, but later admitted to himself that Hinton's son-of-a-bitch stew, sourdough bread, and coffee were well worth the price.

Kelly watched Clayton eat, waited until he built and lit a smoke, and then said, "Tell me about it." He looked at Hinton. "Set, Benny. I want you to hear this."

"You ain't running me out of town, Marshal," Clayton said, more stubbornness than a warning.

"Tell me."

Kelly and Hinton were listening men. They squatted in front of Clayton, waiting, the marshal's head cocked to one side.

"Twenty-five years ago, on the last day of the last year of the late war, a bunch of irregular Reb cavalry rode up on a farm in the Beaver Creek country of northern Kansas."

Clayton drew deep on his cigarette. "They say Frank and Jesse James were with the outfit, but I don't know about that."

"Just say it plain," Kelly said. "Don't tell me what you don't know."

"All right, the telling is simple enough. The Rebs ransacked the farm, took what they could carry, but one of them, a youngster by the name of Lissome Terry, shot the farmer right there in his parlor."

"For no reason?"

"He had a reason. The farmer's young wife was the reason."

Clayton searched his memory, made sure he got the story right. "The farmer's backbone was broke, maybe an inch above his belt. He lay paralyzed on the floor, watched Terry throw his wife on the table and violate her."

"Then Jesse was nowhere near that farmhouse."

Clayton looked at Kelly. "Why do you say that?"

"Because Jesse would have no truck with abusing a woman," Kelly said. "Neither would Frank, even though he was a mean bastard. I rode with them for a spell, back in the day, and I knew them as well as any man."

"I don't know if Jesse was there or not, and it doesn't really matter," Clayton said.

"All right, spill the rest."

"Isn't much left to tell. The Rebs rode away, Lissome Terry with them. The farmer's wife got up from the floor, spat on her wounded husband, and stepped over him. She hanged herself in the barn."

"Spat on him, though. Seems hard," Hinton said.

"I guess she blamed him for not trying to save her. Later it turned out the man was paralyzed from the waist down and couldn't have helped her anyhow."

"Kin o' your'n?" Hinton said.

Clayton blinked again, his answer a long time in coming. "No."

"Then how come you're involved?" Kelly said.

"I have a ranch up Abilene way, or had. Three bad winters wiped me out. Had to pay off my hands and sell what cattle I had left. I was flat broke, down on my uppers. Then a man offered me a job."

"To kill this Lissome Terry ranny?" Hinton said.

Clayton nodded. "Two hundred up front, another eight hundred when the job is done."

"You ever kill a man before?"

"No. I never felt the need."

"How do you know Terry is in Bighorn Point?"

"The man who hired me had the Pinkertons trace him this far. For a few years, Terry left a wide path behind him—murder, robbery, you call it—but then he vanished from sight. He was a hard man to track down."

"Why didn't the Pinks grab him?" Kelly said.

"They said Terry is living in this town under a different name, but they couldn't pin him down further. After one of their agents disappeared, the Pinkertons wanted to investigate further, but the man I work for called them off. He convinced them that Terry, or whatever he's known as now, could get wind of what was happening and scamper."

"So the Pinks backed down, huh?" Kelly said. "That isn't like them. They're bulldogs."

Clayton nodded. "They took some convincing, that's for sure."

"And that's when your man hired you. Terry dead, the Pinks satisfied, no loose ends to tie up."

"That's about the size of it."

"It was the farmer who hired you, huh?"

"Yeah. He's a rich man now, but he's confined to a wheelchair and the pain he lives with every day, inside and out, don't let him forget."

"And you reckon Terry will get wind of you being in Bighorn Point and try to kill you?" Kelly said.

"Yeah, once the word gets out that I'm hunting him. He has no other choice."

Clayton smiled, looked from Kelly to Hinton. "I'm depending on you boys to spread the good news."

"Maybe we will," Kelly said, "after I make up my mind on whether to run you out of town or shoot you."

Hinton looked at the lawman. "Bighorn Point is a peaceful, God-fearing town, Marshal, and this here feller spells trouble. You take my advice and just gun him."

"Your advice is noted, Benny," Kelly said.

The eyes he turned on Clayton were as hard as chips of granite. "I'm still studying on it."

Chapter 4

"Well?" Benny Hinton said after a few moments.

"Well, what?" Kelly said.

"Ain't your studyin' done? Are you gonna gun him?"

"Not just yet."

Clayton felt anger in him, hot and red as a

flaring match. He rose to his feet. "Marshal, I told you I've never killed a man, but that doesn't mean I don't know how to use a gun."

Kelly hadn't moved. He squatted on his heels, smiling, his hands still.

"Mr. Clayton, you'd just think about skinning the iron and then you'd be dead."

He rose to his feet. "I don't plan on killing you anyhow. At least, not tonight."

"You lettin' him stay on, Marshal?" Hinton said.

"For a week."

Kelly looked at Clayton. "If you ain't dead in seven days, then you leave town. That set all right with you?"

"Ask me again in a week," Clayton said. "I'll give you my answer then."

Kelly recognized the implied challenge, ignored it. "You got a week, and that's all you got."

"Damn it, why, Marshal?" Hinton said. "There ain't no bad folks in this town. This stranger is a bounty hunter. He might shoot anybody he pleases, then gallop back to Abilene and claim his reward."

"He's no bounty hunter, Benny. I can smell one of them from a mile off. No, he's what he says he is—a one-loop rancher down on his luck—and he's got seven days to find his man. If that man even exists."

"I asked you why afore. Now I'm asking it again," Hinton said.

Kelly's head turned slowly in Hinton's direction. "Because I'm bored, Benny. Bored with this damned town, bored with my do-nothing job, bored with you and four hundred respectable citizens just like you."

The old man was stung, and for a moment his thinking slipped a cog. Anger can push a man into dangerous territory, and Hinton stepped over that boundary.

His cheekbones burning, he said, "Or maybe you've slowed down on account of them years of doin' nothin' and you think this stranger can shade you with the iron."

A second passed, another. Kelly stood stock-still. Then he moved.

His hands blurred and suddenly the Bulldogs were hammering, his bullets kicking up straw and dirt around the old man's feet.

Hinton screamed, did a frantic jig, then fell flat on his back.

Talking through the ringing echoes that followed, Kelly said, "Still fast enough for you, Benny?"

"You're crazy!" the old man shrieked. "Plumb loco!"

Kelly grinned. "No, I'm not crazy. Like I said, I'm bored."

Clayton heard shouts, and doors opened somewhere in the street outside.

The marshal, still grinning, stepped to the barn door and held up his hands.

"Go back to bed, folks," he yelled. "Just some plumb loco rooster shooting at the moon."

"You all right, Marshal?" a man's voice said.

"I'm fine. Now go home, and take them others with you."

After the mutterings of his would-be rescuers faded into silence, Kelly turned in the doorway and looked at Clayton.

"Did you think that was fast, Mr. Clayton?" he said.

"I've never seen faster," Clayton said.

"Hell, and I wasn't even half trying," Kelly said.

Chapter 5

Cage Clayton woke after an hour of restless sleep.

Kelly was gone and Hinton had locked himself in his office, making a point of slamming the bolt home so Clayton would hear it.

Clayton glanced at his watch. It was two thirty, the dead of night. He rose, dusted straw off his pants, and stepped to the livery door. The town was quiet, sleeping under a lilac sky aflame with stars. The air smelled of pine, carried on the wind off the Sans Bois Mountains a few miles to the south, and to the north, out on the prairie, night birds called into darkness.

Clayton walked a few yards away from the barn and looked down the shadowed street. Somewhere out there was a man who would try to kill him.

Not tonight, but maybe the day after or the day after that.

He lit a cigarette. He knew that if he stepped out of line, Nook Kelly would gun him. But where was that line?

Only the marshal knew, and he wasn't telling, at least not yet.

Kelly told Hinton he was bored, wanted to see what would happen. But when it did happen . . . what then?

Clayton might have to kill a man Kelly didn't want dead. The little gun exhibition he'd given tonight wasn't really directed at Hinton. It was a warning to Clayton: *Cross me and I'll kill you.*

The rancher's cigarette had gone out. He lit it again, the match flame reflecting orange on the lean planes of his face. Clayton had no crystal ball. He couldn't predict the future. But one thing he did know—he could never match Nook Kelly's skill with a gun. Not in this lifetime or in any other.

He ground out the cigarette butt under the sole of his boot and shook his head. All he could do now was take things as they came. There was no use building barriers on a bridge he hadn't even crossed yet.

Yet, as Clayton lay again on his uncomfortable bed of straw and sacking, a man was already plotting his death.

He didn't know it then. But he would know it soon.

Chapter 6

"He's here. The man you said would come."

Two figures were silhouetted in the dark room. One on his feet, one sitting up in bed.

"Bounty hunter?" the man in the bed said. His voice was the weak whisper of a man who found it hard to breathe.

"Rancher. Or so he says."

"How do you know?"

"Egan Jones, the ferryman. Rode into town on a lathered mule, maybe an hour ago, to spread the news. Kelly told him he already knew, so Jones came here, figured you'd want to hear it."

"He did right. But he knows too much, that damned ferryman, or guesses too much."

"You want me to get rid of him permanent?"

"No, not yet. Give him ten dollars and tell him to keep his big mouth shut."

"Sure."

"What's this man's name?"

"I don't know. He didn't give Jones his handle. Said he was from up Abilene way, though."

"Then this has got to be the work of that Kansas farmer, damn him to hellfire and perdition. How can a man nurse a hate for twenty-five years?"

The man in the bed grabbed a bottle from the table beside him and rattled two pills into his hand. His tall companion poured him water and watched as the sick man palmed the pills into his mouth.

He lay back on the pillow, his voice even weaker now. "You'll get rid of him?"

"Of course."

"I want it done quickly and quietly. Oh, and let the Fat Man know you're taking care of the situation. One other thing: Make it look good for Kelly. I don't want him on the prod."

"I got rid of the Pinkertons. You hear anybody complain, Kelly included?"

"No, you did well and helped me repay a favor."

The sick man on the bed raised a white hand with blue veins. "Lee mustn't know about this. I want her kept well out of it."

"She never found out about the Pinkertons."

"No, she didn't. So do the same with this stranger from Abilene."

"A good thing Lee doesn't know about our other . . . enterprise. I hope no one ever feels the need to tell her."

"Who would tell her?"

"I might, if it was to my advantage."

"You wouldn't dare."

"Old man, push me hard enough and I'll dare."

A silence stretched between the two men; then the tall man said, "I still want her."

"I'll see you in hell first," the man in the bed said.

"One day, when I'm ready, I'll take her."

"She wants nothing to do with you. She set her sights higher than Texas gun trash when she married me."

"I can make her change her mind."

The bed creaked as the older man leaned forward, peering into the gloom. "Touch my wife and I'll kill you."

The tall man moved to the door and looked back. "You'll kill nobody, you damned cripple. Just remember, I can wring your scrawny neck like a chicken anytime I feel like it, or spill the beans to Kelly and have him do it with a rope."

"And you'll swing with me."

The tall man smiled, his teeth a white gleam in the darkness. "It might be worth it to see you dangle at the end of a rope."

A sudden fear gripped the man in the bed. Best to play for time. Pretend a small surrender. "We'll talk. Kill the man from Abilene and then we'll talk."

"Damn right we'll talk. When I want a woman I take her and I won't let her husband or her daddy or the Devil himself stand in my way."

The right hand of the man on the bed rested on the walnut butt of a Colt. And for an instant he tensed, ready.

But the moment came and went.

He couldn't kill this man. He needed him too badly.

After the man from Abilene was dead . . . well, there would be time enough.

"Don't fail me," he said.

"Have I ever failed you before?"

The tall man slammed the door behind him.

Chapter 7

A slamming door woke Cage Clayton. Benny Hinton stood over him, grinning.

"Figured that would wake you up."

"You always slam doors so loud?"

"Only when I want to wake fellers I don't like to see sleeping in my barn."

Clayton rose to his feet and stretched, working the kinks out of his back. He took time to build and light a smoke, then said, "Is there a place where I can get breakfast?"

"Sure. Mom's Kitchen and Pie Shop, just down the street a ways."

"Is that all she sells, damned pies?" Clayton was in a sour mood and his back and hips ached.

"No, Mom will cook you up a good breakfast, steak and taters, if you can pay for it."

"I'm buying Mr. Clayton breakfast this morning."

Nook Kelly stood at the barn door. He was freshly shaved, his dragoon mustache trimmed, his clothes clean and pressed.

To Clayton's disgust the lawman looked bright-eyed and bushy-tailed, as though he'd spent the last ten hours sound asleep in a feather bed.

"You ready?" Kelly said, smiling.

"Give me a minute," Clayton said. "I ain't hardly awake yet."

He washed his face and hands in the horse trough and used his bandanna to dry off. He settled his new hat on his head, then ran a forefinger under his mustache. "Now I'm ready," he said.

"And you're surely a joy to behold," Kelly said.

"Kelly, I'm surprised nobody ever shot you for being so damned cheerful in the morning," Clayton said.

"Just my sunshiny good nature coming up with the dawn."

"Go to hell," Clayton said.

"Hinton said Mom's Kitchen is the best place for breakfast," Clayton said.

"Yeah, he would, since he's sparking the old gal."

Kelly neatly avoided a pile of horse dung on the street, then said, "The Windy Hall serves a good breakfast and the coffee is the best in the Oklahoma Territory."

Kelly constantly touched his hat brim to the respectable ladies of Bighorn Point, and prosperous businessmen called out to him by name.

"No whores in this town, huh?" Clayton said.

"Who told you that?"

"A ferryman back a ways."

"Ferrymen talk, but they don't know squat," Kelly said. "The Windy Hall has what it calls hostesses. As to whether they're in the business or not, you'd have to ask when you run up on one."

"I'm just curious, is all."

"Or looking for trouble."

"No, just curious."

Clayton stopped at the door to the saloon.

"Kelly, why are you doing this, buying me breakfast like we were kissin' kin?"

The marshal smiled. "Because you're where the action's at, Mr. Clayton. Bighorn Point had lost its snap before you arrived. I think that's all about to change."

"Can't you call me Cage?"

"No, I can't."

"I'm a big eater," Clayton said. "Your bill will run high."

"Then let's eat, shall we?"

The Windy Hall was narrow, dark, and dingy, cringing in on itself as though apologizing for being in such a God-fearing town in the first place. The reason for its name became quickly apparent to anyone entering—owing to some peculiarity in its construction, the prairie wind sighed around its roof constantly, a low, soft moaning, like a widow mourning a husband.

As Kelly had promised, the food was good, the coffee better. When he finished eating, Clayton pushed himself back from the table, burped, and built a cigarette.

"That was good," he said to Kelly.

"Figured that. You ate enough for three grown men."

"You're paying, so I figured, what the hell?"

"Did you like the waitress?"

"Yeah. She's right pretty."

"Then don't like her. Her boyfriend is sitting over yonder and the look he's giving you ain't exactly social."

Clayton let his eyes drift to a table set against the far wall of the saloon. Two men sat there, one picking his teeth with a fork.

"The one on the left," Kelly said, "giving you the hard eye."

"I see him."

"Name's Charlie Mitchell. He claims he killed a man in El Paso and another in Wichita. Fancies himself a fast gun and wants to be known as a hard case."

"He's too young to be the feller I'm looking for," Clayton said, dismissing the man.

"Yeah, but he's not too young to kill you," Kelly said.

Chapter 8

Nook Kelly, more experienced in the ways of the wannabe gunfighter, saw it coming down before Clayton.

Mitchell leaned across the table and said something to the man picking his teeth. That man, small and mean with the face of a ferret, looked over at Clayton and laughed.

Mitchell said something else and the ferret shrugged and said, his voice loud, "Hell, he wants your woman, Charlie. He made that clear."

The ferret said it and Kelly heard it.

He turned to Clayton. "Bad stuff coming down."

"Looks like," Clayton said. "But I have no quarrel with that man."

"He has a quarrel with you, though."

"Can you make it go away?"

"Yeah, I can kill him. You want that?"

"I can't step away from this, can I?"

"Oh, I don't know. Charlie is no bargain. Some fellers would."

"Some fellers can't hold up their heads in the company of men either."

"I can stop it. Just say the word."

Clayton shook his head. "If it comes, it's my play. I'll go it alone."

"Suit yourself. But I've seen Charlie shoot. He's good."

"You ever seen me shoot?"

Kelly made no answer and Clayton said, smiling, "I'm not good. At least, that's what I think."

"Your gun's back at the livery."

"Didn't think I'd need it this early in the morning. Anyhow, you were here to protect me."

"Trusting man, ain't you?" Kelly said

Mitchell was on his feet. He was a tall, muscular man, somewhere in his midtwenties. Back along the line, he'd decided to affect the dress and manner of the frontier gambler. He wore a black frock coat, boiled white shirt with a string tie, black-and-white-checkered pants and a low-crowned flat-brimmed hat.

"Charlie keeps his gun in the right pocket of his coat," Kelly whispered. "And he'll probably have a hideout in a shoulder holster."

"Ready for war, ain't he?" Clayton said.

"Only with you," Kelly said. The marshal grinned. "Damn it, Mr. Clayton, even without trying, you make things happen. You surely do."

Mitchell walked to Clayton's table, his boots thudding on the wood floor. There were a dozen men and a few women in the saloon, and now Mitchell addressed them.

"You've all heard about this man." He pointed at Clayton. "He says he won't leave Bighorn Point until he's killed one of our citizens, man, woman, or child."

"Shame," a woman said. She looked at Clayton. "For shame."

"Well, I'm giving him his chance," Mitchell said. He looked down at Clayton. "I'm a citizen of this town. Let's see you try to kill me."

"You tell him, Charlie," a man said, a giggle in his voice.

Kelly rose to his feet. "Charlie, this man is unarmed," he said. "Draw down on him and I'll hang you before sundown."

"You in on this, Nook?" Mitchell said.

"Keeping it fair, is all."

Mitchell turned and called out to the ferret, "Wilson, give him a gun."

The man called Wilson strode to the table. He wore two Colts, slung low in crossed belts.

Clayton grimaced. *Another damned tinhorn.*

Wilson laid a short-barreled Colt on the table and Mitchell sneered, "You got a gun now, mister. You bragged you'd kill a woman or child. Well, let's see how you stack up against men."

The bartender and pretty waitress had moved out of the line of fire and a silence, taut as a fiddle string, stretched across the sun-slanted saloon.

Mitchell had a hand in his coat pocket. "Pick up the iron and get to your work," he said. "And damn you fer a yellow-bellied coward."

Clayton said nothing, his head bent, staring at the oiled blue steel of the revolver on the table.

Seconds ticked past. . . .

34

Beside him, Clayton heard Kelly groan, a lost, disappointed sound. Sensing faintheartedness, he'd stop it soon.

But Mitchell would not let it go so easily. He took a step toward Clayton, right leg forward, and readied himself to cut loose a backhanded slap across the older man's face.

Mitchell knew what would happen. He could see it, almost taste it.

He'd slap the stranger around, make him bloody, then run him out of Bighorn Point. He'd be a hero, a fearless gunfighter who stood up for his town. Hell, they might even erect a stat—

Clayton's right boot found its target.

The two-inch leather heel, hardened into the consistency of iron by years of sun, snow, wind, and rain, slammed hard into Mitchell's right kneecap.

The man screamed, staggered back. But Clayton was on his feet, crowding him. As Mitchell's gun came out of his pocket, Clayton drove a work-hardened right fist into the man's chin.

Mitchell went down like a poleaxed ox, his back crashing so hard onto the wood floor the bottles behind the bar jumped.

But Wilson was drawing.

Clayton dove for the table and, before it collapsed under him, palmed the blue Colt. He landed on his right side, rolled. Wilson was four feet from him. The little gunman fired first. Too fast. The bullet kicked up pine splinters inches from Clayton's head.

Clayton shoved the Colt out in front of him, thumbed off a shot, then a second.

Hit twice, one of them in the belly, Wilson shrieked and went down, black blood frothing into his mouth.

Mitchell, his right kneecap shattered, was hurt bad, but still game.

He scrabbled around the floor, found his Colt, and tried to bring it into play. Clayton, on his feet now, stepped through smoke and raised his gun.

But Kelly ended it. He kicked the gun out of Mitchell's hand and yelled, "Damn you, Charlie. It's over. He'll kill you."

Mitchell groaned and lay on his back, his right leg from the knee down jutting out at an impossible angle.

But Clayton's blood was still up. His ears ringing from the concussion of the guns, he waved his Colt around the openmouthed crowd and hollered, "I've never harmed a woman or child in my life. Let any one of you bastards step forward and call me a liar."

But only Kelly took that step. He laid a hand on Clayton's shoulder and said, "It's over. You won, so let it go."

Without waiting for an answer, Kelly called to the bartender, "Clem, Hennessy brandy. And two glasses. Damn, I need a drink."

Chapter 9

"Charlie Mitchell will be stove up for weeks," Kelly said. "Doc Sturgis says his kneecap is broke into three pieces."

"And Seth Wilson?" Clayton said.

"Dead as he's ever gonna be. Hell, you know that. You pumped two bullets into him."

Kelly studied Clayton's face. He figured the man was around forty, about the same age as himself, but right now he looked years older.

"It's no easy thing to kill a man," Kelly said. "It happens so fast. Two seconds, maybe less, and a healthy young man is on his way to meet his maker."

Clayton made no answer and Kelly spoke into the silence. "How do you feel?"

"About what?"

"Don't try to buffalo me, Mr. Clayton."

"All right, then—empty. I don't feel a damn thing."

"You will later. Unless you're a natural-born killer, you'll feel that big empty hole inside you and wonder how you can ever fill it again."

Clayton rose to his feet and stepped to his hotel room window. "I'm not that," he said. "Not a born killer."

"Never took you for that. Never pegged you for a killing man."

Without turning, Clayton said, "I do feel something. I feel I should head back to Abilene."

"What about the eight hundred dollars you said would save your ranch?"

"I don't want to step over the bodies of dead men to get it."

"You figured you could just ride into this town and proclaim to all and sundry that you planned to kill a man before you left."

Kelly stepped beside Clayton. "A threat like that can pile up bodies real fast."

"So I found out this morning."

"You can't leave anyhow. You're already in too deep. The man you came down here to kill knows all about you by now. He'll never let you leave the territory alive."

"Why would he care? Just so long as I'm gone."

"You might come back. Whoever the man is, he can't take a chance on you."

Clayton watched a loaded freight wagon rumble past on the street, its huge wheels and the oxen hauling it kicking up a cloud of yellow dust. Over on the opposite boardwalk, a small boy rolled a hoop and a pair of the local belles strolled by, wearing tiny hats, flaunting huge bustles.

"Do you think Charlie Mitchell was paid to set me up?" Clayton said.

"Nope. I think Charlie braced you just for the hell of it and to build his reputation as a pistolero. He picked on the wrong man, was all."

Kelly turned away from the window and stopped at the door. "I'm planting Seth Wilson out at the old army graveyard at sundown when it gets cooler," he said. "Do you want to come pay respects to your dead?"

Clayton hesitated only a moment, then said, "I'll be there."

Kelly nodded. "Good. It's a true-blue thing to do. A town ordinance says I have to be there. You don't."

The old cemetery lay hidden among the Sans Bois foothills, in the shadow of Hulsey Mountain. Its markers were long gone, victim to time and harsh weather, and the place had a run-down, seedy appearance, overgrown and overlooked.

"It's the closest we got to a boot hill," Kelly said as he and Clayton rode up on the place. "They say one of old Geronimo's wives is buried here, but I don't know about that."

The undertaker, a hopping black crow of a man, met them at the sagging iron gate that led into the place. He had a spring wagon drawn by mules and two assistants, men who leaned on their shovels, smoked pipes, and didn't want to be there.

The undertaker handed Kelly and Clayton mourning garments, and asked, "Will there be more?"

The marshal shook his head. "We're it, Sam. Get him planted. Be dark soon."

"Do you plan to guard the body, Marshal?" Sam asked.

Kelly shook his head. "No. He'll have to fend for himself."

The burial ceremony was brief. Sam said the words, the grave diggers smoked their pipes and waited, and the wind slapped the black cotton of the mourning garments against the legs of Clayton and Kelly.

It was full dark, the moon rising, when the last shovelful of dirt fell on Seth Wilson's pine box.

"Let's go," Kelly said.

"Hold up, Marshal," Sam said. He pointed to his assistants. "Are you sure the mayor didn't say anything about paying one of these men to guard the grave?"

Kelly said he hadn't.

Then one of the grave diggers said, "Don't make no difference anyhow. Neither of us is staying." He spat into the dirt at his feet. "If the resurrectionists come after the stiff, they'd leave with two bodies instead of one an' count their blessings."

Sam looked crestfallen, the wind tangling in his beard. "I plant them, the resurrectionists dig 'em up." His eyes sought Kelly's in the gloom. "Don't seem fair, do it, Marshal?"

Kelly smiled. "Life ain't fair, Sam. Nobody should know that better than you."

The undertaker nodded. "True, so very true." A

talking man by nature, he said, "Why, look at young Mrs. Brown, the poor little creature, gone at such a tender . . ."

But Kelly and Clayton had already shed the mourning garments and walked away, leaving Sam to talk into uncaring darkness.

Chapter 10

The two men rode in silence for a while; then Clayton said, "What the hell is a resurrectionist?"

"Fancy name for a body snatcher."

Clayton's face showed his surprise. "I thought all that was over."

"The hell it is. There's a steady market for stiffs in the medical schools back east, and they pay well."

"I reckon Seth Wilson's body would smell pretty high before they got it to New York or Boston or wherever."

"Not if was loaded into a refrigerated railroad car." Kelly turned and looked at Clayton, his face a blur in the crowding darkness. "There's a spur line of the Denver and Rio Grande to the north of town, ends up at a small freight yard. Some of the local ranchers ship cattle from there and occasionally the trains have a passenger car.

"I rode up there one time and saw a bunch of men loading long packing cases into one of them new refrigerator cars I was talking about."

"You figure they were shipping bodies?"

"Sure of it."

Clayton laughed, the first time in a long while, and it felt good. "I didn't know so many folks died around these parts."

"They don't," Kelly said, "at least not white folks, but plenty of Apaches do."

"Apaches?"

"Yeah, starving or dying of disease up there in the mountains."

"So somebody is making money shipping dead Apaches to medical schools back east."

"That's about the size of it, only the Apaches say their people are mysteriously disappearing, especially women and children. They can't account for that and I got to say it's troubling me some."

Kelly's face was grim. "All we need in these parts is another Apache uprising. A few years back Geronimo raised enough hell around here to last white folks a lifetime."

"Did you inspect those packing cases?"

"No. I'm only a town marshal and I was way off my home range. I wired the county sheriff and he told me to forget the damned Apaches and keep an eye on the graves of white folks. The United States Marshal's office said pretty much the same thing."

"The army?"

"Stretched too thin. They already have all the

work they can handle, and disappearing Apaches is pretty low on their list of priorities."

"Take a lot of dead Apaches for a man to make a living at it."

"It's a sideline, I reckon. If you're already shipping beef, why not throw in a few dead bodies and make yourself some extra bucks? Unlike cows, you don't have to feed and care for Apaches, so it's all profit."

"Hell, Kelly, I thought you said you were bored," Clayton said. "It seems to me like there's plenty breaking loose around these parts."

"Maybe so, but it doesn't concern me. If Apaches are murdered and shipped east like sides of beef, it's happening outside my jurisdiction. Take one step beyond the town limits of Bighorn Point and I'm nobody."

Kelly's horse tossed its head, the bit chiming. "So you see, Mr. Clayton, I am bored. Or at least I was until you rode into town."

Chapter 11

Cage Clayton rose with the dawn. He was hungry, but had no desire to eat in the saloon again. That left Mom's Kitchen and its uncertain culinary arts, but it was the only restaurant in town and he started to cross the street. He almost never made it.

He heard the pounding of a horse team's hooves

43

and suddenly a speeding buggy was almost on top of him. Clayton jumped out of the way, tripped, and came down hard on his back. He had a fleeting impression of a pair of galloping grays, a beautiful young woman at the reins, and beside her a small frightened black girl clinging on for dear life.

"Get out of the way, you idiot!" the woman yelled at Clayton.

Then she was gone, the careening buggy lost behind a billowing cloud of dust.

Dazed, Clayton slowly became aware of another face, also female, not beautiful, but pretty enough in a tanned, freckled kind of way.

"Are you all right?" the girl asked.

"I think so," Clayton said. He rose gingerly to his feet. "I don't seem to have any broken bones."

"You're lucky," the girl said. "That was Lee Southwell. She thinks she owns the whole county."

Clayton smiled, rubbing dirt off his pants. "She always drive like that?"

"Always. I heard she's killed three horse teams in the last year."

"How many pedestrians has she killed?" Clayton said.

The girl smiled. "Probably a lot."

Clayton retrieved his hat and settled it on his head. He extended his hand. "Name's Cage Clayton."

They shook briefly. "I'm Emma Kelly. I've heard of you, Mr. Clayton. Somehow I expected somebody bigger and a lot meaner, like an outlaw—" The girl blushed. "Oh, I'm sorry. I didn't mean—"

"I know you didn't," Clayton said, smiling. "I guess you heard why I'm in Bighorn Point and expected some kind of scary bogeyman."

"Something like that."

Suddenly the time and inclination for talk faded.

Clayton tried to fill the void. "I was just about to have breakfast. Would you care to join me?"

"Sorry. I can't. I work in the hat shop and I have to get back. I just popped out when I saw Lee Southwell nearly run you over."

"Well, some other time?" Clayton said.

"Yes. I'd like that. Some other time." The girl lifted her skirts and hurried back to the hat shop, and only the memory of her perfume lingered.

Now that he no longer needed to hide behind his manly pride, Clayton arched his back and groaned away his aches.

Damn, that had hurt.

Mom surprised him.

A pretty, matronly woman with a large bust and an ass an axe handle wide, she served Clayton a hearty breakfast of buttermilk pancakes, steak, and eggs, washed down with excellent coffee. As she refilled his cup, the woman said, "I saw what happened on the street."

Clayton nodded. "An accident, was all."

"I never like to speak ill of anyone," Mom said, "but Lee Southwell is a bad one. If she'd killed you she wouldn't have lost a night's sleep over it."

She glanced around the restaurant, saw that everyone was fully occupied eating or talking over their coffee, and said, "She's married to Parker Southwell, a cripple twice her age. He owns the biggest spread in the territory, and some say he's into some mighty shady dealings."

Clayton's interest quickened.

Could Parker Southwell possibly be the man he was looking for?

He tiptoed around the subject.

"Mrs. Southwell is a beautiful woman," he said.

Mom nodded. "She's all of that, and Park dotes on her. Jewels, clothes, fine horses—what Lee wants, Lee gets."

"Lucky woman."

"Maybe, but she still has to sleep next to an old man with rotten legs and cold hands."

"How long has Park Southwell been in the territory?"

"He was here when I opened this place, and that was ten years ago."

"And before that?"

"Your coffee's getting cold," Mom said.

The woman turned away, poured coffee for a

couple of middle-aged drummers, then stepped back to Clayton's table.

"Park Southwell isn't the man you're looking for," she said. "And if he was, you'd never get past his foreman." She studied Clayton's face. "Name Shad Vestal mean anything to you?"

"Can't say as it does."

"He's a gunfighter out of Texas and fast on the draw, though he doesn't boast of it. Some say he's faster than Nook Kelly, and some say he isn't. Maybe one day those two will go at it and settle the argument, but until then, you step wide around Vestal and Park Southwell."

"Seems like sound advice," Clayton said.

Mom said, "Yes, and here's some that are even sounder—get the hell out of Bighorn Point and never come back."

Chapter 12

Fate is not content to inflict one calamity on a man; it loves to pile them up.

Clayton had dismissed his run-in with Lee Southwell from his mind, but now it came back to him with a vengeance.

The woman stood on the boardwalk outside the hat shop, beating the small black girl he'd seen beside her in the buggy. Lee's riding crop rose and fell, cracking across the girl's back. The woman's face was flushed with anger, her mouth pinched,

47

white-rimmed with a cruelty bordering on sadism.

Clayton could not stand still and watch anyone, man, woman, or child—or animal for that matter—abused. The little girl was screaming, begging for mercy, but still the riding crop *whop . . . whop . . . whopped* on her back.

Clayton's long stride thudded on the boardwalk.

As he got closer he heard Lee yell, "You yanked my hair in there, you stupid little—" She raised the crop again, but Clayton's arm shot out and his strong hand closed on the woman's wrist.

"Enough," he said. "She's had enough."

Events were cartwheeling past Clayton at a dizzying speed, but his overloaded brain had time to register a strange fact—the street was crowded, but no one stopped. People quickly passed the scene on the boardwalk, their eyes averted.

Did Lee Southwell instill that much fear?

He had no time to seek an answer. Displaying amazing strength, the woman had already wrenched away from him.

A split second later, the crop slashed across his left cheek and Clayton felt blood splash hot on his skin.

"How dare you!" Lee shrieked. "You laid hands on me."

"Leave the girl alone," Clayton said.

"Why, you . . . you piece of trash!" The riding crop swung again, this time aimed at Clayton's eyes.

He had never struck or abused a woman, but there's a first time for everything. Avoiding the blow, he moved in quickly, effortlessly picked Lee up, and stepped off the boardwalk. Under the saloon hitch rail, there was a deep puddle of dung and horse piss. He carried the woman there and dumped her in the middle of it.

Lee slapped facedown into the pungent mess, tried to rise, slipped, and tumbled onto her back. Now the woman was beyond rage, beyond reason. Her hands dripping filth, she opened the small purse she carried and came up with a Remington derringer.

"You bastard!" she screamed, and fired.

The bullet missed.

Using both hands this time, Lee cocked the derringer, her killing eyes never leaving Clayton's face.

She fired at the man from Abilene again.

Another miss.

Frustrated, the woman threw the gun at Clayton's head. He dodged it easily.

"Lie in the piss, Mrs. Southwell," he said. "Cool off for a spell."

"My husband will kill you for this," the woman said, no longer screaming, her voice flat, an ominous sound, like a copperhead rustling through dead grass.

"If he does, I'll hang him for murder."

Nook Kelly stood, stone-faced and terrible, his

49

eyes moving from the woman to Clayton and back.

Kelly raised his gaze to the boardwalk. "Minnie, pick up those packages and help Mrs. Southwell get home."

The black girl shook her head. "I sure won't, Mr. Kelly," she said. "She's done beat me for the last time. I ain't nobody's slave."

The marshal looked at Clayton, at the bleeding cut on his cheek.

He nodded to Lee. "She do that?"

"Cut myself shaving," Clayton said.

"Uh-huh." This time Kelly nodded to the woman sitting up in the piss puddle. "You do that?"

"She needed to cool off, was all," Clayton said.

"I could lock you up for assault," Kelly said. "And you, Mrs. Southwell, for attempted murder."

Lee got to her feet. Her expensive silk morning dress dripped and she reeked of piss and dung.

"But you won't," she said to Kelly. "Unless you want this town burned down around your ears."

"Your threats wouldn't stop me, Mrs. Southwell," he said. "But I think enough damage has been done for one day." He looked at Clayton. "Do you wish to press charges?"

Clayton said he didn't.

"And you, Mrs. Southwell?"

"My husband will press his own charges—at the point of a gun." Her blazing eyes fixed on Clayton. "You're already a dead man."

Kelly smiled. "Good. Now that it's all been settled amicably, I suggest you go home, Mrs. Southwell."

"Minnie, get my boxes and come with me," Lee said.

"No, Miz Southwell, I'm done with you."

"You ungrateful wench, I could—"

"Home, Mrs. Southwell," Kelly said. "I'll send someone to the ranch with your purchases."

"I don't want them now," Lee said. "Give them to charity or burn them. I don't care."

After Lee Southwell left, Minnie stepped beside Clayton. In Kelly's hearing, she said, "Mister, thanks for what you done for me, but you had better get out of town. Shad Vestal will kill you for sure."

Clayton smiled without humor. "You're the second person to tell me that today."

"Good advice is worth repeating," Kelly said.

He wasn't smiling.

Chapter 13

"You think Parker Southwell is the man you're hunting?" Nook Kelly said. He sat down on the hotel bed and made the springs squeal.

"He could be," Clayton said. "I don't know." He smiled. "I'm clutching at straws."

"Either way, Southwell won't forgive you for what you done to his wife."

"Figured that."

"He thinks the sun rises and sets on Lee."

"Heard that."

"And Shad Vestal is hell on wheels on the draw-and-shoot."

"Heard that too."

"I think you should get out of Bighorn Point, Mr. Clayton. I mean the whole town is talking about what you did to Lee Southwell. Everybody was glad to see that uppity snot get her comeuppance, but Park will kill you for it."

Kelly reached out, took the makings from Clayton's shirt pocket, and built himself a cigarette. He waited until the other man lit it for him, then said, "I enjoy having you around, but I don't want you to die for my amusement."

"You told me yesterday that I wouldn't make it out of the territory alive. I think after what happened this morning, my chances are even thinner."

"I can ride with you as far as the Kansas border," Kelly said.

"If Parker Southwell is the kind of man you say he is, he'll track me all the way back to Abilene and kill me there. Or try to."

"If Shad Vestal is after you, he won't try. He'll do."

Clayton made no answer and Kelly said, "Anyway, why I'm here, the mayor wants to talk with you."

"Now?"

"Good a time as any."

"What about?"

"Probably to tell you what a good job you did throwing Lee Southwell in a puddle of horse piss and endangering the whole damn town."

The marshal smiled. "Maybe he's gonna give you a gold medal."

"Kelly," Clayton said, "you got a sense of humor buried somewhere, but I'm damned if I can find it."

"A bad business, Mr. Clayton. Parker Southwell is a vengeful man and I fear the worst."

Mayor John Quarrels leaned back in his chair and talked to the end of his cigar, not Clayton.

"Marshal Kelly told me he's given you a week to find the fugitive murderer and rapist you seek."

"Now it's six days," Kelly said.

"It's not an arrangement I care for, but I will not countermand my city marshal's decision."

Now his cold blue eyes lifted to Clayton. "You know that Mr. Southwell, like your . . . ah . . . employer, is a cripple?"

"Yes, I heard that."

"He tangled with a longhorn three years ago, stove him up badly."

Quarrels, tall, slim, his black hair graying at the temples, was a spectacularly handsome man. He had an air of genteel prosperity. His well-cut gray suit had been tailored in Boston, his spotless linen mail-ordered from Savile Row in London. He spoke softly, a man used to command and the obedience of others.

"The question is, Mr. Clayton, what do we do with you?"

"Help me find the man who was once known as Lissome Terry," Clayton said.

"Whoever he is, he's not in this town," Quarrels said.

"Mr. Clayton thinks Park Southwell could be his man."

Quarrels shook his head. "He's not. Mr. Southwell distinguished himself in the late war as a colonel under General A. P. Hill's command," he said. "He's a brother Mason and true blue."

"But you think he'll try to kill me?" Clayton said.

"Perhaps I can talk him out of it."

"And if you can't?"

Quarrels shrugged. "Then get out of town fast. I'd rather say, 'Here's where Cage Clayton ran' than 'Here's where Cage Clayton died.'" He smiled. "Catch my drift?"

Kelly said, "Make him a deputy, Mayor."

Quarrels was surprised and displeased, and it showed.

But the marshal said, "Swear him in as my deputy for six days. Park Southwell has always respected the star on a man's chest. It might give Mr. Clayton some protection."

"It's thin, Marshal," Quarrels said.

"I can get him out of town for a couple of days until this blows over."

Anger rasped in Clayton's voice. "I'd like to remind you two that I'm still here. I reckon I'm capable of planning my own future, and it doesn't include a star."

"Two days, Cage," Kelly said, using Clayton's given name for the first time. "I'll talk to Park Southwell and then do some rootin' around on my own account. If Lissome Terry is in Bighorn Point, I'll find him."

"And when you do?"

"I'll arrest him."

"Why the sudden change of heart, Kelly?" Clayton said. "I thought you didn't give a damn."

"Maybe I don't, but I'm still a sworn officer of the law. If Terry's here, and you can prove that he done what you say he done, he'll stand trial for rape and murder."

"No matter who he is?"

"No matter who he is."

Mayor Quarrels watched cigar smoke curl above his head. He nodded. "Now that I've reconsidered, I think your suggestion is an excellent one, Marshal Kelly. Deputize Mr. Clayton, then send him out of town. It will give me a chance to talk to Park and his missus and calm them down."

He looked at Clayton. "Well, what do you say? We can do you no fairer."

"Cage, like the mayor said, sometimes it's safer for a man to pull his freight than his gun," Kelly said.

"I still plan on killing Terry," Clayton said. He looked at Kelly. "That's a thing you're going to have to deal with."

"I will, if and when that time comes."

"And I want another week."

Kelly looked for the mayor's reaction, but the man's face was bland, almost disinterested.

"It's a deal, Deputy Clayton," Kelly said.

Chapter 14

Cage Clayton rode north out of Bighorn Point, then followed Sans Bois Creek east until its fork. He splashed across shallow water and drew rein in a stand of willow and cottonwoods.

According to Kelly, the terminal of the railroad spur should be less than a mile ahead, in rolling long grass country.

It was not yet noon, but the day was hot under a hammering sun. Nothing moved and the only sound was the small music of crickets in the grass.

Clayton swung out of the saddle, eased the girth on the buckskin, and let the little horse graze under the trees.

He fetched his back up against a cottonwood

56

trunk, laid his hat on a bent knee, and lit a cigarette.

Around him stretched beautiful country, but it was a lost and lonely land, haunted by the ghosts of vanished buffalo herds and the Indians who had hunted them.

Clayton smiled. Kelly knew what he was doing. Nobody would look for him out here. This was the end of the earth and the beginning of nowhere.

"If you get the chance, see what's in them packing cases in the refrigerator cars," the marshal had told him. "Maybe it's only beef, but it could be something else."

And Clayton had smiled at the man. "You're making busywork for me, right?"

Caught in his own deception, Kelly grinned. "Well, I don't reckon you're going to find dead Apaches. But you never know."

"And it will keep me out of mischief."

"Two days, Cage. You can stick it out that long. I'll pack you plenty of grub and a bottle of Old Crow, unopened, mind."

"Will you have Terry when I get back?"

Kelly shook his head. "I don't know. But I'll try my best to find him."

"Man can't say better than that."

"Keep safe out there, Cage. I don't think Vestal will discover where you're at, but you never know."

"Maybe he'll wish he hadn't—if he finds me, I mean."

"Cage, Shad Vestal can shade you any day of the week, without even half trying."

"I'm that bad, huh?"

"No, you're pretty handy with a gun. You proved that in the Windy Hall when you killed Seth Wilson, but you're not in Vestal's class. But then, few are."

Kelly laid a hand on Clayton's shoulder. "Remember that and you'll live longer."

Now, pleasantly drowsy among the trees, lulled by the creek's soft song, Clayton knew his best option was to ride north and forget the whole sorry business.

But he realized that was impossible.

There was one thing about him that Nook Kelly didn't know—the force that drove the man called Cage Clayton. . . .

He was filled with hate.

That's why he wouldn't back off, from Shad Vestal or anybody else. Hate is like water in a dry gulch: The longer it runs, the deeper it digs. And Clayton's hate was deep . . . the product of twenty-five years, a hate so intense, so painful it afflicted him like a disease.

He rose to his feet, tightened the buckskin's cinch, and swung into the saddle. To the south, purple clouds were forming over the peaks of the Sans Bois, and the wind had picked up, carrying with it a distant rumble of thunder.

It would storm before too much longer.

Clayton took a yellow slicker from behind his saddle and laid it over the horn. He allowed himself a smile. Maybe he wasn't ready for much, including Shad Vestal, but he could still beat the rain.

Clayton topped a rise and saw the railroad spur ahead of him. Beside the single track were a water tower, a woodpile, and an old boxcar that had been converted into a makeshift station house. A handful of men moved around down there and he backed off. He rode down the rise, dismounted, and slid his Winchester from the boot. Slowly he inched back to the crest and dropped on his belly in the long grass.

Two mounted cowboys watched three Mexicans load sides of beef, wrapped in thin burlap, into one of the new Swift refrigerator cars.

The loading, from two heaped wagons, took the best part of an hour, since the beef had to be carefully packed into the bottom of the car where the air was coolest. The cowboys didn't help. If they couldn't work from the back of a horse, they didn't work. But they were happy to supervise, encouraging the sweating Mexicans to greater effort with regular kicks up the ass.

After the car was packed, another wagon drove up to the spur. An elderly Mexican handled the four-mule team, and a couple more men sat in the back.

The wagon was loaded with boxes made of

rough, unfinished pine, and these were man-handled into the car.

Clayton touched his tongue to his dry top lip. Kelly had sent him here only to kill time and stay the hell out of the way. But he wanted to look inside those boxes.

Was there beef inside—or dead meat of a very different kind?

Chapter 15

The rain came as the day shaded into evening, and with it thunder and sizzling streaks of lightning.

Clayton shrugged into his slicker, then topped the rise again. Down below at the spur, the work was over. The cowboys were riding away, followed by the wagons. He waited for another ten minutes to make sure no one was coming back, then got to his feet and walked down the opposite side of the rise.

Rain pounding him, Clayton reached the refrigerator car, then stopped, his breath catching in his chest. Above the roar of the storm, footsteps crunched on gravel.

A few moments passed; then Clayton heard a foot skid on the wet grass beside the track and a man cursed. Clayton leveled the Winchester and stepped into the shadow of the car.

The footsteps stopped, as though a sixth sense

had warned the man that there was someone close, in the darkness.

"Tom, is that you?" the man said. A listening moment, then, "Lon?"

Thunder filled the silence and lightning gave it authority.

Clayton heard a triple click as the man cocked a Colt.

"You come out now," he said. "I don't let bums ride this train."

Clayton took a couple of steps out of the shadows. "Deputy Marshal Cage Clayton out of Bighorn Point," he said, talking into a dark wall, needled with rain.

"Fur piece off your home range, ain't you, lawman?" the man said.

"Some."

"Step toward me, real slow," the man said. "I got faith in this here hog leg, day or night."

"I'm not hunting trouble," Clayton said. Then, "I got me a rifle."

"Lay her down, show your honorable intentions, and then walk toward me."

Clayton hesitated, and the man said, "Hurry it up, Deputy. I'm a railroad employee, but they don't pay me to get wet."

Clayton laid the rifle at his feet and walked into the darkness. A split second later he saw the orange flash of a Colt. The boom of the gun and the impact of the bullet came together.

Hit hard, Clayton took a step back, his hand clawing for the gun under his slicker. The man fired again. A miss.

"You dirty bastard!" Clayton roared, and shot at where he'd pegged the gun flash to be. He fired again.

He heard a groan, then the heavy thud of a body falling on the ground.

Stumbling forward, lashed by rain, he almost stumbled over the man's sprawled form. He kneeled by the body, pushed the muzzle of his Colt into the man's left eye and said, "Damn you, mister. You'd no call to do that. No need to cut loose at a man who was doing you no harm."

But he was talking to a corpse.

Both Clayton's bullets had hit the man square in the chest, the wounds so close he could have covered them with his hand.

The dead man was wearing a railroad guard's uniform. He was not young, somewhere in his early fifties, but, even in death, hard and cruel in the face.

Clayton rose to his feet and looked down at the man.

"I'd say you've shot your share of bums and Chinese coolies off'n your trains," he said. "Only I'm not one o' them. Your mistake, feller."

Suddenly Clayton felt the pain of his wound. His left thigh was covered with blood. Mixed with rain, it ran over his boots and pooled rust red on the ground under him.

Limping, his eyes squeezing against the pain, he picked up his Winchester, then stepped around the refrigerator car and crossed the tracks.

The door of the old boxcar by the water tower was partly open, and a rectangle of lamplight splashed on the wet ground outside.

Moving slowly, carefully, Clayton walked to the boxcar and stepped inside.

There was a partition wall to Clayton's right, probably to separate a storage area from the guard's sleeping quarters. A stove glowed cherry red in one corner, and there was a table and two benches and an iron cot, pushed against the far wall.

Coffee simmered on the stove top; beside the pot, a small frying pan.

Clayton looked at the pan. It held strips of bacon, not yet too badly burned, and a slice of fried bread.

Limping, he looked around and found a tin cup. He poured coffee and walked both cup and pan to the table.

There was a hole in his leg that looked bloody and raw, but no bones seemed to be broken.

After he'd eaten and smoked a cigarette, he'd go back and get his horse. When he dug the bullet out of his thigh, he'd need that bottle of Old Crow.

Clayton let out a long, deep sigh.

He didn't need anyone to tell him that he was in a helluva fix.

Chapter 16

Parker Southwell rolled his wheelchair to his wife's bedside.

"How are you feeling, my darling?" he said.

"Look," Lee Southwell said. She held up her right arm. "Look at the bruise the brute left on my wrist."

"He'll pay for it, my dear," Southwell said. "Soon he won't be around to trouble you anymore."

Lee smiled. "Park, you're so kind and loving. What did I ever do to deserve a husband like you?"

"You were in Denver at the same time I was," Southwell said. "What would you call that? Fate? Serendipity?"

Thunder crashed overhead and Lee shivered, pretending a fear she did not feel.

"The thunder won't harm you, my love," Southwell said. "I'll let nothing or no one harm you, ever again."

Lee picked up a corner of the silk bedsheet and dabbed at the corner of her eye. She sniffed and said, "Does it ever trouble you, Park?"

"Does what trouble me?"

"That you found me in a . . . a house of ill repute?"

"Why, of course it doesn't, my love. That was then—this is now. All I think about is our future together."

"I was no good, Park." Lee buried her face in her hands. "I'm so ashamed. . . ."

Southwell gently pulled his wife's hands away. "There's no shame. As far as I'm concerned, you were a virgin on our wedding night."

Lee pretended to bravely hold back tears. "I wish I could go back, to before we met," she said. "I would have saved myself for you, Park. Just for you to treasure."

"I have enough. I have you."

Southwell's hand moved up until it touched Lee's left arm. He squeezed. Much too hard. Painfully.

Lee winced, but did not pull away.

He could be like this, her husband, cruel, wanting to hurt.

Southwell moved his wheelchair closer.

Lee smiled and pulled back the sheet in invitation. "I'm ready for you," she said.

No, I'm not. I don't want your cold, skinny hand crawling all over me like a spider, the stink of your breath, your dead legs between my thighs. . . .

Someone rapped on the door.

Relieved, and before her husband could respond, she called out, "Come in."

Lon Clyde, one of the hands, stepped inside and removed his hat. He spoke to Southwell.

"Boss, Shad Vestal is back."

"Well, man, don't just stand there gawking at my wife. Did he get him?"

"I don't know."

"You're an idiot. Send Shad to me."

Vestal stepped inside a couple of minutes later. He looked dusty and trail worn, his face gray with fatigue.

"Well?" Southwell said.

"He's not in Bighorn Point."

"Damn it, I know that. Kelly made him a deputy and sent him away somewhere to hide him from me."

"I searched as far west as Robbers Cave, thinking he might be there," Vestal said. "He wasn't. Then I swung south to Limestone Ridge, then Blue Mountain."

Vestal shook his head. "No luck. It's like he's vanished off the face of the earth."

"I want that man dead, Shad. Saddle yourself a fresh horse and get back on the hunt."

"It's dark. I can't find a man in the dark."

"Yes, you can. He's a rube and he'll light a fire. Head north this time. Find him."

"Shad," Lee said, "track Clayton down just for me. And when you get him, take your time killing him. I want him to know he's dying."

"Well, don't just stand there," Southwell said. "You heard my wife: Kill the son of a bitch."

Vestal nodded. "Just as you say, Park."

He and Lee exchanged a single glance, but it was one that held memories of shared pleasures past and the promise of many more to come.

"That man is as big an idiot as the rest of the hands," Southwell said after Vestal left.

Lee said nothing. As her husband's hand went to her body again, squeezing, twisting, Lee consoled herself with one exquisite thought. . . .

Soon she'd kill the old man who was so greedily pawing her, spittle gathering at the corners of his mouth.

And then she and Shad would be free.

And rich.

Chapter 17

By the time he had retrieved his horse and staked him out on a patch of grass among some wild oak, Cage's leg had started to bleed again and the pain was a living thing.

After he returned to the old boxcar, he tried to numb the searing pain with the Old Crow, but he couldn't drink too much, not if he was to dig out the .45 ball buried in his thigh.

Clayton opened his Barlow knife and poured whiskey over the carbon steel blade. He dropped his pants; then, as careful as a naked man climbing over barbed wire, he shoved the point of the blade into the open wound.

Clayton bit back a scream.

Oh God, I can't do this.

His courage wasn't up to the task, and that was

the long and short of the thing. He gritted his teeth.

Cage, you damn coward, get it done. There ain't nobody but you.

He plunged the knife deeper, and this time he screamed. He reached out, grabbed the Old Crow with a trembling hand, and gulped down nearly half a pint. The bourbon danced around in his head for a while, then hit him hard.

"Bastard!" Clayton yelled, but whether at the man who'd shot him, the whiskey, or the bullet, even he couldn't tell. He rammed the blade into his leg again.

"Ah! Ah! Ah!" He drank another slug of booze. Deeper. Blood spurted. The pain was white hot. His body shrieked at him to stop. Deeper still. The steel scraped on . . . something. The bullet? Bone? He didn't know. He levered the tip of the blade upward.

"Ah! Ah! Ah!"

More whiskey. Damn, the bottle was almost empty.

Dig down, tip the blade upward.

"Ah! Ah! Ah!"

He saw it! The bullet, a gray iris in a scarlet eyeball. He shoved the blade under the ball. Gritted his teeth. *Now! Tip it up and out!*

The bullet jerked from of the wound, described an arc in the air, and landed with a thud on the floor. Clayton didn't hear it.

He'd already fainted.

• • •

When Cage Clayton woke, he was lying on the floor, the top of his head wedged tight against a wall.

How long had he been out?

He looked at his watch. It had just gone on three o'clock and the night was still full dark. An hour, then, maybe less.

He rose slowly to his feet, the wound in his leg paining him like blazes. A quick search of the room uncovered a clean white shirt left by its recently deceased owner.

Hungover, his head pounding, Clayton poured himself a cup of coffee, then sat at the table again. The wound looked red and inflamed, but it had stopped bleeding. He drank coffee, then built and lit a cigarette, steeling himself for what he had to do.

He picked up the Old Crow. Good, there was enough left. Now wasn't the time to hesitate. Clayton poured the contents of the bottle into his open wound.

He roared as shrieking pain slammed at him, coming in waves, each one more agonizing than the one before.

This time he didn't faint, but he vented his lungs.

"Aaaarrrgh . . . ya son of a bitch!"

It took him time to recover, but after a few minutes Clayton used the shirt to bind his wound.

He stood, gingerly tested the leg. It took his weight, but the pain was considerable.

He sat again, smoked a cigarette, and drank more coffee.

Then he heard the train whistle.

Chapter 18

There was a real possibility that more hard cases were on the train, and Clayton knew he was in no condition to fight anybody. Pain had sapped his strength, and the Old Crow had turned on him and was no longer his best friend.

He rose, looked around the room, then picked up his rifle and staggered outside. Lightning still flashed across the sky, lighting up the clouds, and the rain was still coming down hard, hissing like a dragon in the dark.

Limping badly, he stopped and looked along the tracks. The approaching locomotive was a point of light in the distance, but under his feet the rails were thrumming to the rhythm of its wheels.

Clayton walked around the refrigerator car and dragged the dead guard's body into the underbrush. The effort fatigued him and for a minute he stood with his back against the side of the car, breathing heavily. Then he pushed himself to round the car again and go back to the tracks.

The train seemed no nearer, but the whistle was

louder, its five notes echoing through the rain-lashed hollow of the night. Clayton hesitated, then made up his mind.

It was now or never. He was going to see what was inside those damned boxes. The guard had been ready to kill to keep their secret, so the contents were precious to somebody.

His hearing reaching out to the train, Clayton opened the car. It smelled of meat and blood and ice. And death.

His wounded leg would not allow him to climb inside, but a box, smaller than the others, was near him. He dragged it closer and used the toe of his rifle butt to hammer it open.

The cheap thin pine splintered and Clayton pulled a piece free. He thumbed a match into flame and looked into the box.

A child stared back at him with wide black eyes.

Startled, Clayton took a step back. He heard the clack of the locomotive's wheels, and its whistle again pierced the night. He leaned over the box again and lit another match. In the shifting yellow light, he saw the dead face of a little girl, black hair falling over her shoulders. She wore a buckskin dress that somebody, her mother probably, had decorated with blue Apache beads.

The girl showed no sign of physical violence, but when Clayton looked closer, he saw that she'd vomited down the front of her dress.

The child had been poisoned.

She'd been given something to eat or drink and it had killed her.

A sickness in him, he did not have the time or desire to check the remaining boxes. He had a good idea what they contained.

He laid the splintered pine plank back on top of the box, then slammed shut the car door. As quickly as he could on his bad leg, he stepped away from the tracks and quartered back to where his horse was tethered. There, among the trees, he would not be seen by anyone from the train.

The locomotive huffed on the tracks as it took on water and wood. From his hiding place, Clayton watched a man step inside the boxcar office. He'd left the bourbon bottle, and hopefully all the blood he'd spilled was hidden by the table.

The man was inside only for a minute or so, then reappeared. He laughed and said something to the engineer, then helped hitch the locomotive to the refrigerator car. As Clayton had hoped, the man had seen the bottle and figured the guard had wandered off drunk somewhere.

Clayton sighed his relief. Another gun battle was the last thing on earth he needed. After the locomotive left with the refrigerator car, Clayton returned to the office. The stove still burned with a good heat and wearily he stretched out beside it. Despite the nagging pain in his leg, he slept.

Clayton was unaware that just a mile away, the man who was hunting him was wide awake, listening, watching, a dangerous predator who was one with the unquiet night.

Chapter 19

Shad Vestal sat his horse, head raised, testing the darkness for sound. A pair of hunting coyotes yipped back and forth, and in an oak grove off to his left an owl asked its question of the night. The wind whispered, thunder grumbled in the distance, and raindrops ticked from the tree branches. But there was nothing of human origin. No cough or snore or cry torn from troubled sleep.

Vestal grimaced. Damn it, where was Clayton?

He eased his horse forward, rode through a saddleback between a pair of shallow hills, then up a low ridge, drawing rein near the rain-slicked surface of a volcanic boulder, fallen there a long time past.

Vestal listened, and the night listened to the listener, as though on alert for what he might say or do. Again Vestal lifted his head, smelled the air, trying to scent his prey. He sniffed, sniffed again. No, he had not been mistaken. It was wood smoke, fleeting, faint, but there.

Lightning flashed without thunder, searing the sullen land with stark light. The rain had been heavy earlier, and a man could not build a fire in the open. That left only the boxcar at the railroad spur.

Had Clayton gone there, seeking shelter from the storm? If he had, he was probably dead by now. Hugh Doyle was on guard there, and he was a man inclined to shoot first and ask questions later.

After a last glance at the featureless sky, Vestal swung his horse toward the spur.

When Vestal reached the tracks, he dismounted and switched from boots to moccasins, better for killing work than high heels and spurs.

Even in the dark, he read the story in the bloodstains alongside the rails. The rain had washed some of the blood away, but there was enough left to color scarlet the small pools among the grass and rocks. Two men had fought with guns here. One had been wounded, how badly Vestal couldn't tell. But the other had been hit hard and bled out.

So Doyle had taken a bullet, but had gunned Clayton. That's how he read it.

Like a wolf, Vestal sniffed, his lips drawn back from his teeth. He followed the scent. The body had been dragged into brush close to the tracks. But it was Doyle's corpse, not Clayton's. Vestal pondered that.

Hugh Doyle, one of the railroaders in Park Southwell's pocket, had been good with a gun.

He'd killed two men that Vestal knew about, and enough Chinese to populate a small village.

Clayton was better than he'd given him credit for, handy with the iron. Not that Vestal was afraid—he wasn't—but it was always good to know your enemy.

He drew his Colt and walked toward the boxcar on cat feet. The door was closed and a ribbon of smoke came from the stove's iron chimney. Clayton's horse was grazing nearby.

Vestal paused outside the boxcar for a long minute, listening, but hearing nothing. Clayton was either asleep or dead. Vestal cocked his revolver and slid the door open. It moved without a sound.

The room was lit by a single oil lamp and the glow of the stove. An empty whiskey bottle sat on the table. Clayton lay near the stove, unmoving.

Damn it, was the man already dead?

Moving on silent feet, Vestal stepped to Clayton and stood looking down at him. The man was still breathing.

Vestal lowered the Colt until the muzzle was just an inch from Clayton's temple.

He grinned.

Like taking a candy stick from a baby. . . .

Chapter 20

But Shad Vestal did not pull the trigger. Something was wrong. He eased down the Colt's hammer. Better to kill Clayton later, he thought, on the Southwell Ranch.

Vestal smiled. Yeah, why not? The plan dawned on him with crystal clarity. First, gun the old man, then Clayton. Next, blame Clayton for Park's murder. The man from Abilene thought he'd found the man he'd been hunting and killed him. It was so simple.

He even knew how the newspapers would play it. *Brave ranch foreman Shad Vestal,* they would say, *caught Clayton in the act of trying to violate helpless Mrs. Southwell. Enraged, Clayton went for his murderous revolver, but Shad Vestal was faster on the draw. Now the frontier is rid of yet another mad-dog killer and would-be rapist.*

Then the clincher: *Mrs. Southwell, at present heavily sedated, will inherit the Southwell ranch and all of her dead husband's business interests.*

Vestal felt like giggling in sheer joy. The plan was so perfect . . . so faultlessly rounded. A thought occurred to him then. Why not kill Clayton now and take him back to the ranch draped over his horse?

He shook his head. No, that was too messy.

Suppose he met someone on the trail, Kelly

76

maybe? He would have some explaining to do. He'd get out of it, of course, but why take the chance?

No, he'd follow the plan as it had come to him, take Clayton back to the ranch and kill him there.

Vestal rammed his foot into Clayton's ribs.

"Get up, you," he said. "We're riding."

Chapter 21

Cage Clayton awoke to pain. He looked up at the flashily handsome man towering over him. "Who the hell are you?"

"Name's Shad Vestal."

"You found me?"

"A blind man could've found you. On your feet."

Clayton staggered upright, his eyes moving, searching for his chance. He found none. Vestal was as aware as a hunting wolf.

"I can't get up. I'm shot through and through," Clayton said. "Took a bullet in the thigh."

"Then I'll gun you right here," Vestal said. "Your choice."

"Where are you taking me?" Clayton said.

He felt weak and light-headed from loss of blood, but he pretended to be more frail than he was and frightened to death—though the latter wasn't much of a stretch.

"You're going to the ranch. Mr. Southwell wants

to talk to you about dumping his wife in a pool of shit."

"I'm sorry about that."

"Sorry don't cut it."

Vestal's hand moved like a striking snake and removed Clayton's gun from the holster. "You kill Hugh Doyle with this?"

"The guard?"

"Yeah, him."

"Yes, I did. He didn't give me much choice."

"Was he trying?"

"His best, seemed like."

Vestal shoved the Colt in his waistband. "Don't even think about it with me. I'm a lot better than Doyle."

It went against the grain and made Clayton queasy deep in his gut, but he played the whining coward role to the hilt. If Vestal didn't respect him, he might get careless. "Listen, Mr. Vestal, let me go," he said. "I've got money, and you can have it."

The big gunman showed a flash of interest. "Where?"

"Back in Abilene."

"How much?"

"Eight hundred dollars."

Vestal laughed. "Hell, Clayton, dead, you're worth a hundred times that."

"I don't understand."

"Mister, you don't need to understand. All you got to do is die."

Clayton played for time. When Vestal was talking, he wasn't shooting. "I know about the Apaches."

"Know what?"

"That you or Park Southwell is shipping their bodies to medical schools back east."

Clayton didn't know who was responsible for the Apache deaths. He was taking a stab in the dark, playing for time.

Vestal smiled. "Nobody cares about Apaches."

"The law might."

"And who is going to tell them?" Vestal's voice was flat with threat.

Clayton had backed himself into a corner. Now he tried to get out of it. "Not me, Mr. Vestal. I won't tell anybody."

"Damn right you won't."

The gunman picked up Clayton's rifle and stepped to the door of the boxcar. He glanced outside, then came back to the stove. "Be light soon. We'll wait till then."

He took the cup from the table and poured himself coffee, holding the Winchester under his arm. "Sit," he said.

Clayton limped to the table, grimacing. He wanted Vestal to think he was hurt worse than he was. Again, given the gnawing pain in his leg, that didn't stretch his acting skills.

Vestal laid the rifle on the table and put his foot on the bench. "Get this into your thick head,

Clayton. Nobody cares about Apaches, living or dead." He waved a hand. "Out there on the range, times are hard. Cattle prices are low and we've had some bad winters—lost a heap of cattle."

"I know all about that," Clayton said, trying to find common ground with the gunman. Maybe it would make him less inclined to shoot right away.

"An Apache on the hoof is worth nothing," Vestal said. "Dead, he brings five hundred dollars on the Boston and New York medical markets."

"Including the children?"

"Especially the children. The doctors like them young and fresh."

"You . . . you just kill them?"

Vestal shrugged. "I prefer to say we process them, just like beef."

"How much can a man like Southwell earn from dead Apaches in a year?"

"Depends. But in an average year, I'd say ten to fifteen thousand dollars. And that's all profit. You don't need to feed Apaches." Vestal grinned. "And we dig up the occasional newly buried body to add to the take. Maybe we'll even process you."

A faint mother-of-pearl light filled the boxcar's open doorway.

"Saddle up, Clayton," Vestal said. "It's time to hit the trail."

"Do you still aim to kill me, Mr. Vestal?" Clayton said, again playing the frightened innocent.

The gunman nodded.

"There ain't much a man can depend on in this life, but you can depend on this," he said. "I surely am going to kill you."

The fear that twisted in Clayton's belly wasn't pretend. It was all too real.

Chapter 22

"You're up early this morning, Marshal," J. T. Burke said.

"Thunderstorm kept me awake," Kelly said.

"They will do that."

The marshal's eyes roamed around the newspaper office, an inky shambles of scattered file cabinets, type cases, discarded sheets of newsprint, composing stones, and a huge platen printing press.

"J.T., I'd like to read your files going back, say, ten years or so," Kelly said.

The proprietor of the *Bighorn Point Pioneer*, a tall, thin man with an alcoholic flush and one arm, made an apologetic face.

"Sorry, Marshal. My back issues only date from 1886," he said. "Everything before that burned in a fire. I rebuilt this place the year before you became the law here."

"Damn it," Kelly said.

"My memories didn't burn," Burke said. "The misuse of whiskey has dulled them some, I admit, but maybe there's something I can help you with."

The editor's eyes sharpened as he sensed a story.

Kelly knew Burke was as slippery as an eel and would come at him from a direction he didn't expect, wheedling out information before he even knew he was giving it. He threw up a defense, a disinterested casualness. "I just had some time to kill and figured I'd find out what happened in Bighorn Point before I became marshal," he said.

Burke's eyes were still probing. "Nothing happened," he said. "The town was dying, breathing its last."

Kelly saw an opening, and he took it. "So, what changed things?"

Burke opened a desk drawer and held up a pint of whiskey. "Drink?"

"No, thanks," Kelly said. "A bit too early for me."

"You mind if I do? Just a heart starter, you understand."

"Help yourself."

Burke took a swig, put the bottle back in the drawer, and said, "So, what changed things?"

Kelly said nothing, waiting for the editor to fill in the silence.

"Parker Southwell and his partners changed things," Burke said.

"I didn't know he had partners."

"He did, way back when."

Again Kelly waited. He had no clear idea why he wanted information on Southwell, except that Clayton had said the old man could be the one he was hunting. What was it he'd said?

"He could be. I don't know."

So even Clayton wasn't sure. But Kelly had decided to at least go through the motions of finding out.

Burke was talking again.

"Ten years ago, let me see. That would be the spring of 'eighty, Southwell came up the trail from Texas with nine hundred head of cattle and told folks he planned to establish a ranch south of town."

"His partners were with him?"

"Yes, but they weren't cattlemen. One was John Quarrels, our current mayor; the other, Ben St. John, owner of the only bank in our fair city."

"What did Quarrels do?"

"He built a dry goods store but sold it after a year. The mayor is not a man to stand behind a counter in an apron." Burke opened the drawer again, stared inside as though trying to make up his mind, then closed it. "Ben St. John used his own start-up money for the bank, so he must have had quite a stash when he arrived in Bighorn Point," he said.

"So between the three of them, they saved the town from drying up and blowing away?" Kelly said.

"Sure. We had a bank, an excellent store, and a big ranch close by. The next year St. John and Quarrels bankrolled the building of a church and a school, hired a reverend and a teacher, and people started to arrive, eager to call such a God-fearing town home."

"How come only one saloon?"

"Southwell, St. John, and Quarrels are the movers and shakers in Bighorn Point, and one thing they wanted was respectability. They closed three of the saloons and left one open as a courtesy to travelers. As Parker Southwell said at the time, 'A saloon has never helped business, education, church, morality, female purity, or any of the other virtues we hold so dear.' "

Burke couldn't resist a sly dig. "Maybe ol' Park should forget cows, grab his Bible, and go on the kerosene circuit."

"Give me an out-and-out scoundrel any day," Kelly said. "I don't much like being around respectable people."

"A man after my own heart," Burke said. "You sure you don't want a drink?"

"I'm sure. I got to be on my way."

"Mr. Clayton—is he respectable?" Burke said.

The question took Kelly by surprise. Burke had a way of doing that. "Why do you ask?"

"Our man from Abilene says he'll kill somebody in this town before he leaves. Is that respectable?"

"No, I guess not."

"Unless he has a good reason?"

"I'm sure he has."

"Avenging a past wrong, I imagine."

"Yeah, it has to be something like that."

"Perhaps Mr. Southwell is his intended target."

Now the marshal was wary. "What makes you say that?"

"Mr. Southwell is a man without a known past."

Kelly smiled. "Hell, J.T., he's been in this town for the last ten years."

"Yes, but what did he do during the time between the end of the war and 1880? Come to that, what did his partners do?"

"Former partners."

"Former? Maybe. Maybe not."

Kelly shook his head. "J.T., you're a suspicious man."

"That's what makes me a good newspaperman, Marshal. Perhaps I'll do some digging, find out what Southwell and the others did in Texas after the war."

"You do that, and when you find out let me know."

Burke opened the drawer and took out the bottle. To Kelly's retreating back, he said, "Mixed brands, Marshal."

Kelly stopped and turned. "What the hell are you talking about, J.T.?"

"I inspected those nine hundred cows Southwell drove up from Texas. They were all young, and they wore a bunch of different brands." He looked at Kelly. "Something to think about."

"Hell, so he bought them from ranches on his way up the trail."

"Or he rustled them," Burke said.

Chapter 23

"The ranch is southwest of town on a creek," Shad Vestal said, drawing rein. "I'd say we're less than an hour away." He looked at Clayton and grinned. "Time to make peace with your maker."

Clayton realized that this man was going to kill him, no matter what, and he dropped all pretense. "Vestal," he said, "you're a yellow-bellied son of a bitch and low down. It don't take much of a man to kill an unarmed prisoner."

Vestal smiled. "Clayton, I'm glad you said that. It will make my job so much easier." The smile slipped and became a snarl. "I was gonna give it to you in the head, but now you get two in the belly where it hurts real bad. Now get off your damned horse."

Vestal's engraved, silver-plated Colt, as flashy as the man himself, was trained on Clayton, hammer back and ready.

Clayton swung out of the saddle. His head spun as he tried to say a prayer, but he couldn't string the words together in his mind.

"Now take three steps away from the horse, then turn and face me."

Clayton did as he was told. "You yellow son of a bitch," he said again, the cuss coming easier than the prayer.

Vestal grinned, his teeth white. "Two just above your belt buckle. You'll scream like a woman. For hours."

Clayton braced himself for what was to come.

Shots hammered, their echoes racketing around the hills. Clayton felt the burn of a bullet; then he threw himself flat on the grass.

He heard the pound of hooves and glanced up. Vestal was galloping away, raking his horse's flanks with his spurs.

Five men on small ponies rode over a notch in the hills and went after him, firing rifles. But the range was too great. Vestal had a much better horse and opened distance between himself and his pursuers.

Clayton caught up his buckskin and had just swung into the saddle when the five men trotted back.

He wasn't going anywhere. The five rifles trained on him made that perfectly clear.

Cage Clayton felt sweat trickle down his back. The day was hot, but he knew this for a fear sweat. He expected the five rifles to blast at him any minute. Nothing happened.

One by one the rifles lowered and he looked into flat Apache faces, angry, hard, and rough-hewn as rock—merciless. One of the riders, wearing a ragged white man's coat and plug hat, grabbed the buckskin's reins. He led Clayton after the others.

There was nothing about this setup Clayton liked. What was the old saying? *Out of the frying pan, into the fire.*

A bullet had burned across the meat of his left shoulder, not deep, but enough to draw a trickle of blood.

The Apaches rode southeast, farther into the Sans Bois. They were grim, silent men and the only sounds were the fall of hooves and the creak of saddle leather.

After an hour along a whisper of trail that switched constantly back and forth around rock falls and steep mountain ledges, the Apaches rode into an arroyo that ended in a tree-covered clearing about five acres in extent.

Clayton heard the sound of trickling water, and a section of the far rock wall of the arroyo, under an overhang, was blackened from countless generations of campfires.

He then had his first indication that the Apaches didn't hold him in high regard. The man leading his horse pulled him alongside, raised his foot, and kicked him out of the saddle. Clayton landed hard on his wounded thigh and groaned in sudden agony.

The stony faces of the Apaches around him told him that the groan had not added any to his prestige. After being hauled to his feet, Clayton was dragged to the overhang and thrown on his back.

An older man, with tired eyes that had seen too much of life and death, kneeled beside him. Like the other Apaches, he wore white men's castoffs. He had the look of a farmer, not a bronco warrior, but his blue headband marked him as a former army scout.

"We will ask questions of you. If you tell us the truth, you will die quickly," the old man said. His hair was gray and thin. "But if you lie, then you will beg the Apache to kill you, because your death will be painful and slow in coming."

Clayton said nothing, no words springing to mind that could get him out of this fix.

"Why do you kill the Apache?" the old man said.

Chapter 24

"I do not kill Apaches," Clayton said, finding his voice at last.

"You were with one who does. The one we call the Hunter."

"I was his prisoner. That's why I have no weapons. He took them from me." He showed the star on his shirt. "I am a lawman."

Another Indian grunted. Whether it was a good or bad sign, Clayton didn't know.

"Why did the Hunter take you captive?" the old Apache said.

"I saw . . . I know what he does with the dead Apaches."

"What does he do?"

"He sells them and they are taken away in a railroad car." Clayton racked his brain, trying to find an alternative to *refrigerator car,* a term these Indians wouldn't know. "It is a car of ice," he said. "Colder than the coldest winter."

That last started talk among the men and their faces were puzzled.

"Why a car of ice?" the old Apache said.

"To take them far to the east, to the great cities."

Damn, how do I explain doctors, vivisection, and medical research to an Indian?

"What do they do with the bodies of Apaches in these great cities? Do the white men eat them?"

"No, they cut them up."

That caused a stir among the Apaches, and the youngest, a teenager wearing a collarless shirt with a red-and-white-striped tie, turned his face to the sky and wailed like a wounded wolf.

"You lie to us," the old Apache said. "You tell us tall tales."

"I do not lie," Clayton said. "Doctors . . . medicine men . . . cut up the bodies to look inside them."

The old man was shaken to the core. His voice caught in his throat and his hands trembled. "If a Mescalero is treated thus, his soul cannot fly to the Land of Ever Summer. He will wander forever in a misty place between heaven and hell."

The Apaches looked into Clayton's eyes. "Can what you tell us be so?"

"It is so," Clayton said. He was aware that he was walking a ragged edge between life and death, and right then he wouldn't have given a plug nickel for his chances.

"Why does the Hunter kill us and send our bodies away?" the Apache said.

"For money."

The old man rose. His face was like stone, but there was an unsteadiness to his chin. The others gathered around him and they talked briefly before he returned to Clayton's side.

Apaches had an inborn contempt and hatred of liars, and the old man showed it now as black lightning flashed in his eyes.

"You are either telling the truth or you are the greatest of all liars," he said. "If you have lied to us, we will tear out your tongue so you can never tell an untruth again."

He grabbed Clayton's hand and, showing surprising strength, pulled him to his feet.

"Have I made our feelings clear to you?" he said.

"I do not lie to the Apaches," Clayton said.

"Then we shall see. You will take us to the car of"—he used *zas*, the Jicarilla word for snow, then corrected himself—"ice. You will show us where the bodies of our children lie."

Clayton's heart sank. "The car is gone. I don't know when there will be another."

"Then I think you are a liar," the old man said.

"I can take you to the railroad tracks where the ice car sits when it comes."

"You will show us."

Clayton nodded.

Suddenly he felt a chill and he knew why. . . .

Death stood at his elbow and was growing mighty impatient.

Chapter 25

"The saber, sharpened to a razor's edge, is the solution to our Indian problem," Parker Southwell said.

"As you say, dear," his wife said.

"Do you think Lo would dare set foot off the reservations assigned to him if he knew ten thousand sabers awaited him?"

"I think not," Lee Southwell said, picking at her food. She had heard all this many times before.

She and her husband sat at opposite ends of the long table that occupied almost the entire dining room. Two black servants stood by to serve them, heads bowed as had been the custom of the old South.

"It is well known that the gallant Custer, on the bloody field of the Bighorn, cried out in extremis, 'Oh, for an 'undred sabers!'"

"I'm sure he did," Lee Southwell said.

Her husband spoke around a mouthful of roast beef. "I wrote to President Harrison and told him—I said, 'There's only one way to gain the respect and obedience of the Indian. Apply the edge of the saber and apply it often. Apply it till it's bloody from tip to hilt.'"

"I know you did, dear," Lee said.

"The man's a bleeding heart, a damned Injun lover. He didn't even answer me."

"His loss, dear."

"Yes, and this great nation's loss."

The evening was hot, the candlelit room was stifling, and there was no breeze to offer relief. Sweat trickled between Lee's breasts and down her thighs, and the heavy silk dress she wore stuck to her back.

She worried about Shad out there somewhere in the darkness. Clayton was a desperate, ruthless man and she hoped Shad had not ridden into danger.

Southwell motioned with his fork. "The roast beef is not to your liking?"

"I'm just not hungry tonight and I have a slight headache," Lee said. She laid her knife and fork on the plate.

"Hester, remove Mrs. Southwell's plate."

Southwell looked at his wife, his thin face distorted by candle flames. "Would you care for something else, my dear?"

"Yes, a glass of bourbon."

"A glass of bourbon, Hester," Southwell said to the black woman.

"Do we have any ice left?" Lee said.

"Yes, ma'am," Hester said.

"Then bourbon with plenty of ice."

Lee had just been served her drink when a servant stepped into the room.

"Mr. Vestal just rode in, Mr. Southwell," the man said.

"Tell him to report to me right away," Southwell said.

"Yes, sir."

Lee's heart sang. Shad was back. He was alive.

Vestal, tall, handsome, with a sweeping mustache and yellow hair falling over his shoulders, stepped into the room a couple of minutes later and Southwell waved him into a chair.

"Well, is he dead?"

"I'm sure of it," Vestal said.

"You mean you don't know?"

"The Apaches have him."

"Apaches! What the hell are you talking about, man?"

Vestal glanced at Lee, then told Southwell about

his capture of Clayton and the attack by the Indians.

"You two leave the room," Southwell said to the black couple.

He waited until they were gone, and turned to Vestal. "That was this morning. Where have you been all day?"

"Well, after a spell I tracked them, thinking they'd shoot Clayton right away. They didn't. They rode into an arroyo. I waited around for a few minutes, then left."

"They tortured him to death, probably," Southwell said.

"That would be my guess."

"A deserved fate for a singularly unpleasant man," Lee said.

"Park, those Apaches were on the warpath," Vestal said, ignoring the woman. "And there could be more of them. I warned you, we're culling them too close, too often."

Southwell shot a quick glance at his wife, then said, "Shut your trap."

Vestal smiled. "Don't you think she knows?"

He looked at Lee. "Cattle prices are low, money is tight. Where do you think the ruby necklace you're wearing came from?"

"Vestal, I warn you—"

"Oh, shut up, Park," Lee said. "I know what you're doing to the Apaches, and I don't care. Did you really think the deaths of a few savages would offend my sensibilities?"

"I was trying to shield you, my dear," Southwell said. "Harvesting Apaches is a dirty business."

Lee lifted the glittering necklace from between her breasts and put it to her nose. "I can't smell any dirt," she said.

Vestal laughed, but when he turned to Southwell again, he was serious. "I think we should end the cull for a while."

Southwell shook his head. "Impossible. I have a hunting party out in the Sans Bois now, and a refrigerator car will arrive at the spur tomorrow night."

"Who's leading them?"

"Baldy Benton—him and Luke Witherspoon."

"I'll go after them, call them back."

"No! Do you want to take a look at my accounts ledger? We need the money, Shad."

He looked from Vestal to Lee, breathtakingly beautiful in the soft light that erased the hard lines around her eyes and corners of her mouth.

"The cull goes on," he said. "Until there are no Apaches left to harvest."

Chapter 26

There was no sign of life at the spur, and no refrigerator cars.

The iron V of the rails shimmered in the afternoon heat, and the air hung heavy on the trees, their branches listless, unmoving.

As he sat his horse between the Apaches, Clayton felt he was carrying the full weight of the oppressive day. The sky was the color of dust, the yellow coin of the sun hazy, as though shining through murky water.

The youngest Apache, the butt of his Winchester on his thigh, rode his paint down the rise to the tracks. He rode to the boxcar, leaned over, and slid the door open. The young Apache looked inside, then swung away and drew rein at the tracks. He stared into the distance: rolling hills, empty land, empty sky.

Clayton sweated, smelled the rankness of his body. Beside him the old Apache yelled a few words and the youth on the paint returned.

The old man turned to Clayton, his black eyes accusing. "No Apaches. No white men. No cars. No nothing."

"The ice car will be here," Clayton said.

"When?"

"I don't know."

The Apache grunted. "Then we will wait."

"It could be a long time, maybe days."

"We will wait." He pointed his rifle at Clayton. "You will wait."

The old man led the way into a stand of wild oak where the Apaches picketed their horses, then sat in a circle in a patch of shade, Clayton with them.

They waited. . . .

To the Apache, patience is the companion of

wisdom. Not passive waiting, for that is laziness, but to wait and hope.

"We will hear the train by and by," the old man told Clayton.

The man from Abilene said nothing. He was hot, thirsty, and hungry, and patience had never been one of his virtues. He lay on his back, the stoical Indians sitting still and silent around him. Clayton stared into the tree canopy, the leaves silhouetted black against the sky as though charred by fire. His brain reeled, hunting the answer to an impossible question: Why had it all gotten so complicated when once it had seemed so straightforward?

His plan had been so simple. Ride into Bighorn Point, declare his intention to kill a man, and let the man's own guilt drive him from hiding. The guilty party would call him out, and Clayton would shoot him.

Instead . . .

Clayton groaned. It hurt his head to even think about it.

The dreary day dragged past with dreadful sluggishness. Then slowly the light seen through the tree canopy changed. Gone was the sullen sky of afternoon, replaced by a million diamonds scattered on lilac velvet.

Clayton sat up. The Apaches hadn't moved, sitting in a circle, thinking . . . about what only God knew. They'd had neither food nor drink, nor had he, but Clayton was irritable and the wound in his thigh throbbed. If he had a woman close, he'd whine and moan and let her comfort him.

The Apaches needed no such comfort. They were like their mountains—still, silent, unchanging, enduring. With that strange sense many Indians possess, the old Apache said something to the youngest one. The youth rose to his feet, stepped to his horse, and returned with a canteen and a chunk of antelope meat.

These he offered to Clayton.

None of the other Apaches were eating or asking for water, a fact Clayton noticed. A man's pride is a personal thing. But in the long run, it's what separates the exceptional from the mediocre. Clayton refused the food.

"I will eat and drink when the Apache eat and drink," he said.

The old man beside him nodded. Then he smiled.

Why he did the last, Clayton did not know.

Two hours later, he heard the rumble of wagon wheels, and after a few more minutes, the distant wail of an approaching locomotive.

Chapter 27

Marshal Nook Kelly stood outside his office, smoking his last cigar of the day. The town was quiet and the street was deserted. A few lights burned in the windows of the houses beyond the church, and over at John Whipple's gun and rod store, his little calico cat explored the night.

Despite the quiet, Kelly was uneasy. Where the hell was Clayton? He should have returned from the spur by now.

The marshal admitted to himself that he liked the man from Abilene. Clayton was a cattleman, not a gunfighter, and he'd found himself out of his depth as a bounty hunter.

When this whole thing with Park Southwell's wife blew over, and it looked as if it had because Kelly had not seen the old man or Shad Vestal either, then he'd send Clayton on home. The man he was looking for was not in Bighorn Point or he'd have revealed himself by now.

Park Southwell didn't shape up as much of a human being, and probably had started his ranch with stolen cattle, but he'd been a colonel in the war, not a guerilla fighter like Lissome Terry.

As far as Kelly was concerned, Southwell was in the clear.

But that didn't answer the question—where was Cage Clayton?

There were outlaws aplenty up here in the Nations, and a few bronco Apaches who hadn't gotten the word about Geronimo. It was a dangerous place for a pilgrim, especially one wearing a lawman's star on his shirt.

Kelly drew deeply on his cigar. Clayton was handy enough with a gun, but a bullet in the back has a way of canceling out that advantage. The marshal shook his head. Hell, he'd sent Clayton out to the spur, and he was responsible for his safety. But then, Cage was a grown man and could take care of himself. And he knew what . . .

"Damn it!" Kelly swore aloud.

The bottom line was he'd sent the man out to the spur and it was his duty as a peace officer to make sure he wasn't in danger.

The marshal pitched his cigar into the street. He stepped into his office, grabbed his rifle from the rack, and blew out the oil lamp.

On his way to the livery stable, Kelly suddenly realized what was at the root of his decision to find Clayton.

"Nook Kelly," he told himself, "you're just too damned softhearted for your own good."

Chapter 28

The Apaches moved through the darkness like silent ghosts.

Clayton joined them on the ridge and looked down at the spur. A single wagon was drawn up close to the tracks, two cowboys riding herd on its Mexican drivers. The train was off somewhere in the distance, but close enough that Clayton heard the *chuff-chuff-chuff* of the locomotive.

Beside him the Apaches were tense, ready. Now

he could only act as a bystander and wait for them to make their move.

A couple of minutes ticked past. The Apaches lay still in the grass, watching. Waiting.

But for what?

Then it dawned on Clayton. They wouldn't make a move until the engine arrived. If there were Apache bodies in the wagon, then God help the train crew.

After what seemed an endless wait, the train arrived. It was a locomotive with a single boxcar—a refrigerator car. The engine vented steam, for a moment obscuring the wagon and the two riders.

The Apaches moved. They crouched low and ran down the slope, Clayton with them. As the steam cleared, the cowboys saw the Indians. And made the last mistake they'd ever make.

Both men went for their holstered guns, and the Apaches fired.

One man was hit in the head and his hat flew off, revealing his complete baldness. He toppled out of the saddle as his companion, hit hard, swung his horse around and tried to make a dash for the trees.

The young Apache drew a bead and shot him, shot him again, and the man fell.

The two Mexicans were wide-eyed with terror. One of them screamed, *"Por favor, no mas mate!"*

The Apaches ignored his plea for mercy and yelled at the engineer and fireman to climb down from the cab.

Their hands in the air, the railroaders stood by the engine. Clayton saw that their fear was just as great as that of the Mexicans. Angry Apaches were not to be taken lightly. And they were about to get angrier.

There were two boxes in the wagon. The Apaches opened them and Clayton heard their roars of outrage and sorrow. Knowing what he was about to see, he stepped to the wagon.

A young woman's body occupied each box. Neither showed signs of violence, and Clayton wondered at that until he caught the smell of rotgut whiskey. Then he knew how the women had been killed. Their abductors had gotten the girls drunk and smothered both of them.

"Lipan," the old Apache said, "coming up from the south."

"Where are their men?" Clayton asked. "Why didn't they protect them?"

"Many Apache no longer fight. The Lipan know their days in the sun are over. White men get father, maybe brother, drunk, then take girls."

Suddenly angry, Clayton limped to the bodies of the dead men. Behind him he heard shots. He turned and saw the Mexicans sprawled facedown in the dirt.

Grabbing hold of the back of the bald man's collar, he dragged him to the engineer and his fireman. "Who is he?" he said. "Who does he work for?"

The engineer, a burly man with iron gray hair and a bristling mustache, shook his head. He looked terrified.

"Honest, mister, I don't know. We were told to bring the refrigerator car here and pick up a couple of boxes." His eyes pleaded with Clayton. "That's how it come up, and it's all I know."

If the engineer did know more, he never got a chance to reveal it. The Apaches jumped on him and the fireman and began to kill them more slowly than the others, with knives, not guns.

Clayton thought the men would never stop screaming. But they did, eventually . . . an eventually that took two shrieking, screaming, scarlet-splashed hours.

The Apaches had no way of destroying the engine or the boxcar, and contented themselves with shooting holes in both.

Clayton was under no illusions. He'd heard that Apaches were notoriously notional, but, judging by the way the cards were falling, his turn was next. In the end they surprised him.

The young Indian brought him his horse, and then they left without a word, taking the wagon with them. One moment the spur had been crowded with Apaches; the next they were gone, as silently and ghostly as they'd come.

The Indians had picked up the dead men's rifles, but Clayton scouted around and found the bald man's Colt. He reloaded, shoved the gun in his holster, then filled his cartridge belt. He left the buckskin near the converted boxcar and stepped inside.

The whiskey bottle was empty, which was a disappointment. After witnessing what had happened to the railroad men, he could've used a drink.

Clayton used wood and kindling he found beside the stove and filled the pot with water from the pump outside. He put coffee on to boil, then sat at the table.

A quick inspection of his thigh told him the wound was not infected, and it showed some healing. It still pained him, though, stiffening his entire leg.

Later he poured himself coffee and built a cigarette, inhaling deeply. The sight of the two railroaders haunted him. How could men get cut up like that, their guts coiling from their bellies, and still live? And their eyes . . .

Clayton heard the chime of a bit as someone drew rein outside. Then, "Cage, you still alive?"

Nook Kelly's voice.

"Just about."

"What the hell happened here?"

"A lot."

Clayton drank some coffee and dragged on his cigarette.

"Step inside and I'll tell you about it," he said.

Chapter 29

Kelly sat in silence until Clayton recounted his capture by Shad Vestal and the Apache attack on the refrigerator car and wagon.

When the other man stopped talking, Kelly poured himself coffee, then said, "That's Baldy Benton and Luke Witherspoon lying out there."

"The names mean nothing to me," Clayton said.

"They work for Park Southwell, or did. Benton was pretty well known, a hired gun from up Denver way. I don't know anything about Witherspoon."

"So it's Southwell who's killing Apaches and shipping their bodies east."

"Seems like." Clayton waited a few moments, then said, "Well?"

"Well what?"

"Aren't you going to arrest him?"

"No."

"Damn it, how come?"

"How do I prove it? We don't have the bodies of the Apache women and that means no evidence."

"Hell, I saw the whole thing. I can testify."

Kelly shook his head. "Cage, your testimony

won't carry any weight in Bighorn Point. As far as the good citizens of the town are concerned, you're a troublemaker who vowed to kill one of their number. And you assaulted Park Southwell's wife. A jury would figure you had it in for the old man and concocted a wild story about dead Indians."

"I still plan to reduce the population by one," Clayton said.

"Which one? You still think it's Southwell?"

"I thought it was him. Now I'm not so sure."

"He was a colonel in the war, won a chestful of medals in a dozen pitched battles. You're looking for an irregular who rode with the James boys." Kelly drank from his cup. "Park Southwell is not your man."

"But he might know who is."

"Yeah, I'd say that's a real possibility."

"I'm heading back to town," Clayton said. "I still have a job to do."

"I'd rather you didn't," Kelly said.

"Why do you say that?"

"Because you're more valuable to me dead."

Clayton stiffened and started to rise to his feet.

"Hell, sit down, Cage. I'm not going to kill you."

"If you aren't, you have a strange way of putting things."

Kelly reached out, took the makings from Clayton's shirt pocket, and began to build a cigarette.

For a moment his eyes seemed distant; then he said, "I have a feeling, a hunch you might call it, that something is coming down."

"What something?"

"I don't know. If I knew, maybe I could act on it, think ahead, like." He shook his head. "I can't say what it is, but it's in the air."

"An Apache uprising maybe? Another Geronimo on the warpath?"

"Not a chance. The Apaches are whipped. They'll bury those women, then go back to work on their farms and try to grow crops from rocks and sand. But they'll be on their guard now, and Southwell won't find pickings so easy."

"Then what the hell could it be, this something?"

Kelly drew on his cigarette, exhaling smoke with his words. "I told you, I have no idea. But I'll know it when I see it."

"And why am I dead?"

"If I spread the word around Bighorn Point that you got shot out at the spur by person or persons unknown, somebody's going to make a move. Maybe the man who was once Lissome Terry."

"What kind of move?"

"Well, he could figure his cover was almost blown by the Pinkertons, then you. He might say to himself, 'The third time could be unlucky.' So he packs up and tries to leave town. And that's when I grab him by the cojones."

"Hell, Kelly, it's thin. Coulds and maybes don't

mean a damned thing. Terry's just as likely to stay right where he's at and brazen it out."

"Yeah, I know. Like I said, I'm acting on a hunch, but a lot of my hunches have been right before."

"And a lot have been wrong?"

Kelly smiled. "I believe I've gotten more right than wrong."

Clayton let that pass, and said, "So, now that I'm a dead man, what do I do?"

"There's a mountain called Tucker Knob a couple of miles to the east of here. A prospector by the name of Zeb Sinclair built a cabin there. It's pretty much a ruin now, but it's still got a roof."

"And Mr. Sinclair won't mind?"

"He's dead. Apaches done for him years ago. Nailed him to his own front door."

"It must be a cheerful spot."

"I'll have someone I trust bring supplies out to you. Just stay put until I come for you."

"And if your hunch is wrong and nothing happens? Do I stay dead? Or for some reason it does happen and then it all goes bad? What then?"

"I don't know." The marshal smiled. "But I wouldn't worry about it."

"I worry about it," Clayton said, irritated.

"Well, if it does go bad, we'll probably both be dead anyway."

"Kelly," Clayton said, "you know how to cheer a man, you surely do."

Chapter 30

The Sinclair cabin lay in a tree-covered hollow at the base of Tucker Knob. It was a dark, dismal place, but as Kelly had pointed out, it did have a fairly solid roof. The marshal had discounted the fact that it had no door, no windows, and its only furnishings were a rickety table, a stool, and a stone fireplace that must have been the late Mr. Sinclair's pride and joy.

Clayton spent an uncomfortable, sleepless night in the cabin, sharing space with a pack rat's brood. Come first light, he stepped outside under a crimson and jade sky and drank from the shallow creek that ran off the mountain. He splashed water on his face, wet and combed his hair, and rasped a hand over the rough stubble on his cheeks. He needed a shave, but his kit was back in the hotel at Bighorn Point.

Clayton saw the rider at a distance, coming on at a trot astride a small horse. He ran into the cabin, strapped on his gun belt, then stepped outside again. He took a quick glance at the flaming sky, swallowed hard.

Dear God in heaven, don't let this be Shad Vestal.

It wasn't.

Even when the rider was still a ways off, Clayton saw it was a girl.

Closer . . .

Yep, a right pretty girl at that.

Closer still . . .

Hell, it was the girl from the hat shop. The one who'd helped him after Lee Southwell sideswiped him with her buggy.

She rode a mouse-colored mustang and had a sack of groceries tied to her saddle horn.

"Howdy," Clayton said, smiling, wishing he'd had a shave.

The girl swung out of the saddle. "Howdy yourself, Mr. Clayton." She held out a hand and Clayton took it. "Nice to see you again."

"And you too."

"I've brought the supplies Marshal Kelly promised."

"Oh yes, thank you. Is there coffee in that poke?"

The girl's freckled nose wrinkled as she smiled. "There sure is."

"Can I interest you in a cup?"

"You bet, Mr. Clayton. I haven't had any coffee yet this morning."

"Call me Cage."

"All right, Cage."

"I . . . um . . . I . . ."

"You've forgotten my name, haven't you?"

"Sorry," Clayton said.

The girl's smile widened, white teeth in a pink mouth. "Well, that's understandable. You were still very shook at the time. Emma. Emma Kelly."

"Of course."

Clayton stood gazing at the girl. Damn, she was pretty. She wore a split canvas riding skirt and a tailored yellow shirt. The red glow of the sky tangled in her hair and touched her cheeks with rouge.

"Coffee?" she said, smiling.

Clayton looked like a man waking from a pleasant dream. "Yes, yes, of course, coffee." He gathered his wits together. "Is it coffee? I mean, coffee it is."

Kelly had thought of everything—a small coffeepot, frying pan, and canned milk that Emma poured into her cup. He had also included tobacco and papers, a welcome addition.

She sat on the stool while Clayton perched precariously on the edge of the table, building a cigarette.

"How long have you known Nook Kelly?" he asked.

"Oh, about three years or so. I was raised by an aunt, and after she died, Nook helped me find a job and a place to live. He's been very kind to me over the years; looks out for me like the big brother I never had."

That last pleased Clayton. "Like a big brother" meant there was no romantic relationship between Emma and the marshal.

The girl's eyes rose to Clayton's. "What will

you do when you find"—she hesitated, changed tack—"when your business in Bighorn Point is done?"

"Go back home to Kansas and make a go of my ranch."

"Is it pretty there, where your ranch is?"

"Well, I think so. My place is on the Smoky Hill River, just south of Abilene. Cottonwood trees shade the cabin in summer and hold back the worst of the winds come winter. Summer or winter, a hush lies on the land like a blessing, makes a man stand back and look and wonder and say, 'This is where I live, and this is where I'll be buried.'" Clayton looked embarrassed. "That was a dumb thing to say."

"No, it wasn't. I'd like to see your land one day."

"And I'd like to show it to you one day."

Emma's eyes dropped and her lashes lay on her tanned cheeks like fans. After a few moments she rose to her feet.

"I must be going," she said. "Nook worries about me."

"I'd like to see you again," Clayton said.

"You will," Emma said. She stepped to the doorway. "Cage, be careful. Since you arrived, I think Bighorn Point has become a dangerous place."

"You've been talking to Kelly."

"I know he feels it, but I feel it too. There's something wrong. It's in the air."

"Take care of yourself, Emma," Clayton said.

"And you, Cage. And you."

After a woman a man cares about walks away from him, she leaves silent echoes behind, empty spaces where she sat, where she stood, and he thinks that nothing can ever again fill them.

Clayton was left with only the lingering scent of Emma's perfume, a memory of meadow flowers, and he felt as though he had found something and then lost it again, a fairy gift that vanished with the rising sun.

Chapter 31

Securely rope-tied to his saddle, Parker Southwell supervised the burial of the dead at the spur.

"Plant 'em deep, boys," he yelled. "We don't want dead men walking." He grinned. "Or talking."

"Damn it, Park, I told you we were culling too close," Shad Vestal said. "Now we got Apaches on the warpath. They're breaking out."

Southwell was angry. "White men did this, not Apaches, and we'll hunt them down and kill them."

Vestal was taken aback. "There's Apache sign all over the damned place. The men who did this rode unshod ponies, and white men don't use knives on their captives. You saw the railroaders.

You got any idea how long it took them boys to die?"

"Is Clayton among them?"

"No. I reckon the Apaches killed him earlier."

"Good." Southwell glared at his *segundo*. "White men, Shad. Get that into your thick skull. This outrage was perpetrated by white men."

"How can you deny that it was Apaches done this?" Vestal said. "Who else would have a motive to kill our men, the Mexicans, and the rail-roaders?"

The two men sat their horses in the shade of the trees. The eight riders they'd brought with them dug graves, and complained plenty about doing it.

Southwell turned to Vestal again, his stare cold, lethal.

"Shad, you're an idiot," he said. "If I tell the Denver and Rio Grande railroad shareholders that Apaches killed their engineer and fireman, you know what they're going to do?"

He didn't wait for an answer.

"They'll squawk like ruptured roosters and they'll complain to Washington that their trains are being attacked by bloodthirsty bronco Apaches. How many senators do you think have shares in the D and RG? More than a few, depend on it."

His face suffused by a barely contained anger, the old man said, "Next thing you know, we'll have the army camped on our doorstep and then the questions will start."

As though he were acting a part in a play, Southwell mimicked a perplexed Yankee voice. " 'Why did our red brothers take to the war trail? Dear me, whatever could have been the cause? Wait. Their women and children were being kidnapped and killed, ye say? Right, we'll get to the bottom of this, and, by thunder, heads will roll.' "

Southwell's thin finger poked into Vestal's shoulder. "How long before they discover that we've been harvesting the savages and sending their bodies east—where at least they're finally making themselves useful?"

Vestal was bright enough to see the problem. And a couple of others. "How are we going to pin the blame on white men? And why would they attack the train?"

"The outlaws attacked the train because they heard a rumor that we were making a secret gold shipment."

"Do you expect people to believe that?"

"Of course. If the lie is big enough, people will believe it. More to the point, the railroad will be happy to swallow it hook, line, and sinker."

Southwell spread his hands, the gesture of a man who thought he was stating the obvious. "Now all we have to do is find the culprits and kill them. Then I can tell the D and RG that the murderers of their men were found and brought to justice."

"Find the culprits? Where? I don't catch your drift."

Southwell smiled, a humorless, skull-like grimace. "I'd guess at this very moment they're holed up at the dugout saloon and hog ranch in Smokestack Hollow. It's a well-known nest of thieves, border riffraff, Meskins, and outlaws of every stripe."

Awareness dawned on Vestal, and his smile was genuine.

But if Southwell had known the real reason for that smile, he would have hung his *segundo* from the nearest cottonwood.

Chapter 32

Smokestack Hollow lay less than ten miles from the railroad spur, and when Southwell and his men rode into the shallow, grassy valley, it was still not yet noon.

Both the saloon and adjoining hog ranch were dug into the side of a hill above a U-shaped rock ridge. In front was a dusty clearing that grew a crop of sand and cactus. A screeching windmill dragged water from unwilling layers of shale and sandstone and a huge pig wallowed in mud spawned from the drips.

As Southwell and his riders watched from the shadowed cover of pines and wild oak, a woman stepped out of the hog ranch, threw the contents of a chamber pot into the dirt, then walked inside again.

Someone in the saloon picked on a guitar and a man's yell was joined by the high-pitched female shriek that passed for laughter in an end-of-the-line shop like this one.

Southwell turned to one of the men flanking him. "Benny, run on up there and take a look-see," he said. Then, distrusting the man called Benny's intelligence, he added, "I want to know how many armed men and the number of women. Order a drink, pay for it, and keep your eyes open. When you've seen enough, skedaddle back down here."

"Sure thing, boss," Benny said. He was a coarse-skinned man, his face pitted with acne scars.

"Then get it done."

Southwell watched his man ride up to the saloon, swing out of the saddle, and step inside.

"Shad," he said, "do you think the murdering scum in there hear the chimes at midnight?"

Vestal grinned. "Not yet, but they will, I reckon."

Southwell heard one of his men whisper, "What the hell are the chimes at midnight?"

He sighed.

Ignorant scum in there, ignorant scum out here.

Time passed. The sun climbed in the sky and the blistering day stained the shirts of the waiting horsemen with dark patches of sweat.

Chafed by the ropes that held him in the saddle, Southwell tried to ease himself into a more comfortable position, but failed.

Hot, irritated, he said to Vestal, "Where the hell is Benny? He should be back by now."

Vestal's eyes swept the ridge, then the dugouts. There was no sign of life. Even the pig lay still on its side, asleep, covered in dried mud.

Several minutes ticked past; then Benny stepped from the saloon.

Suddenly, Southwell straightened in the saddle, his eyes popping. *No!* The idiot was backing out, his Colt bucking in his hand.

A tall man in a dirty white shirt appeared in the doorway, a gun in his fist. He doubled over as Benny gut-shot him, but then rose onto his toes and emptied his gun into the dirt at his feet before falling on his face.

Benny sprang into the saddle, firing through the open door. He swung away from the saloon and momentarily disappeared behind the ridge. He reappeared and rode hell-for-leather for the waiting horsemen. He savagely reined in his horse, its haunches slamming into the dirt.

"What the hell happened?" Southwell yelled, his face black with anger.

"Hell, boss, I had me a couple of drinks, figured we was gonna kill them all an' I didn't want a good bottle to go to waste," Benny said, grinning.

"Why the guns?" Southwell said.

"Feller next to me spilled his drink on me. I hate to see a body waste good liquor. So I stuck a knife into his guts an' then finished what I was sippin'."

He waved a hand toward the dugouts. "Them in there got kinda mad about the cuttin'. Had to shoot my way out."

"Looks like you killed one man," Southwell said. "How many others are in there?"

"Four white men, a couple of Mexicans, an' three women . . . left."

"Are all the men armed?"

"Damn right they are."

"You idiot, we could have walked in there and killed them real easy," Southwell said. "Now we've got a gunfight on our hands."

"Sorry, boss."

Southwell drew his gun. "Sorry don't cut it, Benny."

He fired and a small red rose blossomed between Benny's eyes. The man tumbled from his horse and lay still.

"Now what?" Vestal asked, after a disinterested glance at the dead man.

"Because of that idiot, we go the hard route," Southwell said. "Shoot our way in."

Vestal turned to his men. "You heard the boss. Let's get it done."

"How about the women?" a man asked.

Southwell grunted and glared at the man. "Any more damned fool questions?"

No one spoke.

"Right, boys! Then let's root out that nest of murderers."

Chapter 33

"Wait!" Vestal said. "There's a better way."

Southwell's irritation grew. The War Between the States had taught him his soldiering, and now it showed. "There's no better way than the cavalry charge."

"Park, we'd have to cross a hundred yards of open ground and we'd run right up on their guns. We can't outflank the dugouts or attack them from above. We'd lose half our men in the first charge and the other half in the second."

Southwell was stubborn, but he wasn't a stupid man.

"Then what do you suggest?" he said.

"The men in the saloon don't know we're here," Vestal said. "We can ride right in there as friends, only we ain't."

"They'll be suspicious of an armed party. I doubt that they'd consider us friends."

"We drape Benny over his saddle, say we heard gunfire and saw him riding away from the saloon. He shot at us, and we returned fire and killed him."

"And now we're doing the right thing," Southwell said, his eyes suddenly aware. "We just wanted the good folks up there in the saloon to know that a killer has been brought to justice."

"Right," Vestal said. "We wait until they lower their guard, and then we cut them down."

Southwell thought that through, then said, "All right, Shad, we'll try it your way." He called to his men, "Throw that fool over his horse. We'll go play good citizens."

A few men laughed as the dead man was tossed over his saddle.

"Forward, boys," Southwell said. Then to Vestal, "Shad, if this doesn't work, I'll have you shot."

"It will work, Park," Vestal said. "Trust me."

Vestal led Benny's horse. Beside him, adding respectability, was Southwell, wearing his expensive English riding outfit.

Vestal called out to the men inside the dugout, but they were wary.

Finally a voice yelled from inside, "What the hell do you want?"

"We had to kill a man," Southwell said. "We think you might know him."

There was no answer from within.

The man Benny had shot lay sprawled in the dust. His pockets were turned inside out and his boots and belt were gone. His bare feet revealed crooked toes with overgrown nails.

A couple of minutes passed; then Vestal said, "Well, if you folks don't want this stiff, we'll take him back to Bighorn Point."

The voice from inside said, "Hold up there. We'll take a look."

After a few moments the door swung open and two men stepped outside. They were long-haired, bearded, and dirty—typical frontier riffraff. But the guns they held were clean enough, and Vestal noted that the man on the right had a repeating shotgun, a Winchester model of 1887. In a close-up fight it could be a devastating weapon.

It was this man who stepped to Vestal's horse.

He was big, well over six feet, and despite the heat, he wore a bearskin coat.

The fastidious Southwell wrinkled his nose. The man smelled like a damned goatherd.

"What you got?" the man asked.

"We were riding past and heard shots," Vestal said. "Then this feller came down off the ridge at a gallop. He saw us and took a couple of pots, so we had to kill him."

The big man grunted. "You done good."

He stepped past Vestal to Benny's horse and lifted the dead man's head by the hair. He glanced into Benny's face and nodded. "That's him all right. He kilt poor Bob Henry over there an' stabbed another one inside."

"Well, we'll be leaving now," Vestal said. "You can keep the dead man's hoss and traps."

"I surely do appreciate that, mister." The big man flashed a brown and yellow smile. "But I'm what ye might call a thankin' man, an' I'd be right grateful if you and the others in your company would let me buy you a drink."

Vestal turned his head and called out to the men lined up behind him, "How about it, boys? Are you thirsty?"

A ragged cheer went up, and Vestal grinned. "This gentleman is paying, so let's belly up to the bar."

Another cheer and the men dismounted, leading their horses toward the dugout.

Vestal looked at Southwell. "Want me to untie you so you can join us, Park?"

The older man shook his head. On horseback he was a colonel. On the ground he was a helpless cripple.

"Bring me a stirrup cup, Shad," he said.

Vestal had never heard the expression before, but he caught Southwell's drift. "Anything you say, boss."

"And, Shad, tie this up. Make it neat. I don't want anything left alive in there—man, woman, child, or animal."

"You can depend on it, Park," Vestal said.

Inside, the saloon was surprisingly large. The area nearer the door was roofed by the hillside itself, burlap sacks stretched across the ceiling to catch dirt and bugs. But the rear had been blasted from rock and formed a wide cave, used for storage and a sitting and sleeping area. It boasted a couple of tables, each with four chairs and several iron cots.

The bar was to the right of the door, a couple of timber boards laid across trestles. The shelf behind held a few bottles, and a barrel of whiskey sat on top of the bar next to a selection of half-washed glasses.

Vestal's gaze swept the room. A man who looked like the proprietor stood behind the bar, dressed in faded finery—a filthy white shirt, string tie, and brocaded vest. The two other white men looked so much like the man in the bearskin coat they could have been brothers.

It was the Mexicans who caught and fixed Vestal's attention. They were dressed like vaqueros in wide sombreros and tight embroidered jackets, but Vestal pegged them as banditos on the scout from somewhere farther south. Both men wore Colts and had careful eyes and still hands.

The Mexicans would be the greatest gun danger, Vestal decided.

No matter, he would kill those two first.

The body of the man stabbed by Benny had been dragged into a corner. The three painted-up women stepped across to join the men at the bar.

Soon the women were laughing with Vestal's men, each of whom seemed to grow an extra hand with every glass of rotgut.

Vestal sipped his own drink and glanced outside.

Southwell sat his horse under a full sun, looking in the direction of the dugout. Hell, he must be dying of thirst out there. Vestal grinned. If he wanted a drink, let him walk inside and get it.

He smelled the stink of bearskin coat before the man joined him.

"Having a good time there, amigo?"

"Yeah, it's a load of fun," Vestal said. "But it ain't gonna be fun for you any longer."

He drew his gun and pumped two bullets into the big man's belly.

The man's expression changed from good humor, to surprise, and then to an odd kind of hurt, as though Vestal had betrayed him.

"Get 'em, boys!" Vestal yelled.

Guns hammered and the two bearded white men went down. The man behind the bar managed to grab a shotgun before half a dozen guns opened up on him, pulping his chest into a bloody jelly.

Thick smoke drifted through the saloon like a fog and Vestal grabbed his opportunity.

The unglazed window's shutters were open and Vestal two-handed his Colt up to eye level and drew a bead on Southwell's skull. He fired.

The man's head jolted to the side, fanning blood, but he remained where he was, tall and straight in the saddle.

Vestal didn't spare Southwell a second glance. He knew he'd fired a killing shot. He'd scattered the old man's brains and that was the end of him. And good riddance.

A woman screamed out of the smoke haze as

Vestal finished reloading his gun. His men were going after the doves now, and that meant every man in the dugout was already dead.

What about the Mexicans?

Vestal stepped toward the back of the saloon and reached the rock cave. Here the smoke was thinner.

The two Mexicans were on their feet, but neither had drawn his gun.

"*Oye, hombre, qué pasa?*" one of the men said.

Vestal smiled. "I'm what's happening." He went for his gun.

The Mexicans were fast, much faster than honest men have to be. But they didn't come close.

Both men were hit hard before they brought their guns to bear. One was dead when he hit the ground; the other, his mouth full of blood, lasted a few seconds longer.

Vestal reloaded, regarded his dead with a dispassionate interest, then turned his back on them. "We lose anybody?" he asked one of the men.

The man nodded to a body lying under the bar. "Sam Ridge. Caught a stray bullet early in the fight."

"Too bad," Vestal said.

He walked outside to where Southwell sat his horse, staring at the dugout with the leaden eyes of a dead man.

Vestal smiled. Lee would be pleased.

Chapter 34

Cage Clayton was disappointed when he made out the rider trotting toward him, elongated in the shimmering heat haze. He had hoped for Emma Kelly. The reality was Nook Kelly.

Clayton stood outside the cabin and watched the marshal ride closer. When Kelly was within hailing distance, he swallowed his letdown and raised a hand. "Howdy."

"And right back to ya, Cage." Kelly drew rein. "You got coffee left?"

Clayton nodded. "Sure do. Light and set."

Kelly followed Clayton through the open doorway of the cabin.

"You should've put in a door," he said.

"I got no idea how to make a door," Clayton said. "Even if I had tools, which I don't."

"It's easy. All you need is boards, nails, and a hammer."

"How many have you made?"

"To date, none."

"Then you're no one to be giving advice about door making."

"Maybe, but I reckon I could make one if I needed to."

"I've took to liking a cabin without a door," Clayton said. "Lets the breeze through."

Kelly nodded. "There's always that."

The marshal waited until he was seated on Clayton's only chair, a cup of coffee steaming on the table, before he spoke again.

"Parker Southwell is dead," he said. "Dead and buried."

It took a while for Clayton to register that. Finally he said, "How? When?"

"How—he was shot. When—two days ago over at Smokestack Hollow."

"Who shot him?"

"The way Shad Vestal tells it, a bunch of white renegades attacked a train up at the spur. Apparently they'd heard a rumor that Park Southwell was shipping gold in a refrigerator car."

"We know that isn't true," Clayton said.

"Don't we, though?"

Kelly sipped from his cup, then made a face. "Hell, how old is this coffee?"

"Only a couple of days. So, what happened?"

"Again, how Vestal tells it, they tracked the renegades to a dugout saloon in Smokestack Hollow, the gallant Colonel Southwell tied to his hoss. Fearlessly—Vestal's word, not mine—the old man led the attack on the saloon and got killed in the first charge, him and a couple other men, one of them a fast gun by the name of Benny Petite."

"And the renegades?"

"Wiped out to a man, along with four women that got caught in the cross fire."

129

"It's a pack of lies," Clayton said.

"No, it ain't. I rode out to the dugout and there's blood and bullet holes everywhere."

"And the bodies?"

"Vestal said they buried them, along with Southwell and Petite. I saw the grave and there's surely a bunch of folks down there."

"Why didn't he take the old man's body back to Lee?"

"Too hot, Vestal said. He didn't want to lug Park's body through the heat, said it would end up smelling bad and upset his widow."

"Thoughtful of him."

"Yeah, and damned convenient. Ties it all up nice and tight."

Kelly was silent for a few moments, then said, "Needless to say, Shad Vestal is a hero in Bighorn Point and Lee is acting the grieving widow to the hilt. Now there's talk that the Denver and Rio Grande Railroad wants to erect a statue to the gallant Colonel Parker Southwell outside the church."

"On a horse?"

"Probably."

"Southwell must have known it was Apaches attacked the train, and if he didn't, Vestal certainly would. Why murder a bunch of people in a saloon?"

"Blame Apaches and right away everybody's screaming, 'Uprising!' If the army got involved, questions would be asked, and Southwell's involvement in the body trade could've got him hung."

Clayton thought for a while, then said, "I'm going back to Bighorn Point. I still have a job to do."

"Hell, Cage, there's easier ways to earn a thousand dollars. Rob a bank, for Pete's sake."

"It's not just the money. There's something else, something I never mentioned to you before."

"Ah, now you're getting interesting again," Kelly said, lifting the makings from Clayton's pocket. He began to build a cigarette. "For a while there, you really did start to get boring, Cage. So, let's hear your story."

"You ever think of getting your own tobacco?" Clayton said.

"No."

After Kelly lit his smoke, Clayton began to roll his own.

"What I told you about getting a thousand dollars to kill a man in Bighorn Point is true," he said.

"Ah," Kelly said, a meaningless sound.

"What I didn't tell you was that the woman who was raped by Lissome Terry was my mother."

"Now you've surprised me," Kelly said. "Go on."

"After Ma died, my father retreated into himself.

He became a bitter, remote, and hostile man, obsessed with only one thing: making money. He'd taken refuge in a cold, dark place inside him, and then found he couldn't live happily in his own skin."

"And being crippled didn't help, huh?"

"Not a bit."

Clayton drew deep on his cigarette. "I think he may have blamed me for being in Abilene that day picking up supplies. Maybe I could have made a difference. I don't know. Finally, when I was seventeen, I couldn't bear to stay with him any longer. I rode on down to the Panhandle and signed on as a hand with Charlie Goodnight. Went up the trail three times, kept a distance from whiskey and women, saved my money, and started my own brand by way of Abilene Town."

"Then you went belly up," Kelly said.

"Yeah. Pa sent for me, said he'd give me a thousand dollars to get the Rafter C back on its feet if I'd kill a man."

"Lissome Terry."

"Yeah. Pa said the fact that Terry still cast a shadow on the earth ate at him like a cancer. He said he saw Ma all the time and she looked angry. He said her soul would never rest in peace until Terry was dead."

"How did you feel about Terry back then? Did he stick in your craw?"

"I swore that if I ever ran across the man, I'd kill

him. But I had a ranch to build, and riding on a vengeance trail was no part of my plans."

Kelly ground out his cigarette butt under his boot. "The Pinkertons are damn sure that Terry is in Bighorn Point?"

"Seems like. One of their men got too close and disappeared, and they backed off after that. But they still swear Terry is living in the town."

Kelly rose to his feet.

"All right, Cage, let's go find him," he said.

Chapter 35

The hazy peaks of the Sans Bois smudged the horizon as Clayton and Kelly rode across rolling country in the direction of Bighorn Point. Crickets scratched out tunes among the buffalo and lovegrass and heat lay heavy on the land. Only the mountains looked cool.

Ahead of them, two long ridges crowned with a mix of pine and hardwoods formed a narrow canyon, its floor thick with brush and cactus. As Clayton watched, a covey of bobwhite quail exploded from the brush and fluttered into the air before scattering into the long grass. A stray elk or antelope, he figured. A chance for a shot if he were a hunting man.

Kelly turned his head, looked at Clayton. "When Park Southwell came up the trail from Texas ten years ago, he had two partners with him," he said.

"I didn't know that," Clayton said, surprised.

"Me neither until I spoke with J. T. Burke, the editor of the Bighorn Point newspaper. He says the two men with Southwell were John Quarrels and Ben St. John."

"The mayor and . . ."

"St. John is the only banker in town."

"You think—"

"Yeah, either one could be the man you're hunting." Kelly shrugged. "Well, at least it's a possibility to consider."

"Quarrels . . . it's hard to believe—"

"Men change. Many an outlaw settles down and leads a respectable, churchgoing life."

"And St. John?"

Kelly smiled. "A pillar of respectability. He has a horse-faced Yankee wife who brought her own fortune with her and he's a deacon of the church. As far as I can tell, he kisses babies, don't kick dogs, and he's down on liquor, whores, and gambling."

Clayton, thinking, made no answer, and Kelly said, "Shoot 'em both, Cage, an' then you'll be sure you got the right one."

"That was a joke, right?"

Kelly smiled. "Yep, only a—"

The flat statement of the rifle and the thud of the bullet hitting Clayton's horse happened in the same instant. The buckskin went down as though poleaxed, rolled, and pinned Clayton's leg under the saddle.

He was aware of Kelly charging toward the canyon, his rifle to his shoulder, firing.

Clayton tried to drag his leg out from under the horse, but the jolt of pain in his wounded thigh stopped him. He cursed, then pulled his gun. Kelly vanished between the canyon walls and Clayton heard the thudding echoes of gunfire.

What the hell was happening?

He saw a drift of smoke on top of the ridge to his left and thumbed off a couple of shots in that direction. But he was shooting at shadows and the range was too great for a six-gun. Pinned like a butterfly to a board, he could do nothing but wait.

There was a lull in the shooting that lasted almost half a minute, then two more shots. Then silence.

Clayton again tried to free himself. Pain ripped at him, but he clenched his teeth and pulled harder. But the weight of the horse was too great. He wasn't going anywhere, at least not real soon. Was Kelly dead? Would the bushwhackers come to finish the job?

Clayton didn't want to find the answer to either question.

He had lost his hat when the horse fell, and the sun blasted at him. He managed to reload the Colt from his cartridge belt; then his eyes swept the canyon ridges. Nothing moved and there was no sound.

"Kelly!" he yelled.

No answer.

Clayton swore. Alive, the buckskin was a good horse. Dead, he was a son of a bitch.

"Kelly!"

The returning silence mocked Clayton.

"Kelly!"

A bullet kicked up a startled exclamation point of dirt three feet from Clayton's head.

All right, if you feel that way about it, I'll shut up.

A lone horseman rode out of the canyon, coming on slowly though the shimmering landscape.

Clayton shielded his eyes with his hand, squinting into the distance. There was no mistaking the rider—it was Nook Kelly, his Winchester across the saddle horn. When the lawman drew rein, Clayton said, "Hell, was it you took a pot at me?"

"I sure did," Kelly said. He smiled. "I should've blowed your damned brains out."

Chapter 36

"Damn it, what was all the hollering about?" Kelly said.

"I'm pinned under my horse."

"I can see that."

"Why did you shoot at me?"

"To shut you up. Your girlish screams were annoying the hell out of me."

"Well, you could have killed me."

"Sure I could, but I didn't. Just wanted you to be quiet, was all. Did you really think I'd holler back when I wasn't sure how many bushwhackers were up on the ridge?"

Kelly had been right not to give his position away, and Clayton felt like a fool. "Sorry," he said. "I didn't think about that."

Kelly smiled and nodded. "Maybe you're just not a deep-thinking man, Cage. Pity, that."

The words stung and anger flashed in Clayton. "Instead of lecturing, can you get this damned hoss off me?"

"I think so." Kelly grinned. "I'll study on it for a spell and let you know."

"Go to hell," Clayton said.

Kelly used his own mount and a rope to pull Clayton's horse off his leg. It was an efficient way to move the buckskin, but hardly gentle.

"That hurt like hell," Clayton said after he was freed.

"No bones broken, but your wound has opened up again. Looks like you're a bleeder, Cage."

Clayton ignored that and said, "What happened in the arroyo?"

After he took the makings from Clayton's pocket, Kelly started to build a smoke.

"There were two of them," he said, looking down at tobacco and papers. "I've seen them hanging around town for the past month, a couple of young, drifting farm boys down on their luck."

"You killed them both?"

"Yeah. They didn't give me any choice. Those boys were sodbusters, not gunfighters, but they were man-grown enough to carry Winchesters and they used them pretty well."

"Well enough to kill my horse," Clayton said.

"Better the horse than you, I guess."

"Yes. Thank you for that."

"Don't mention it," Kelly said. He smiled at Clayton. "You may not know the man you're hunting, but he sure as hell has you pegged."

"The bullet was meant for me?"

Kelly lit his cigarette and shook out the match. "Now, what do you think? I'm a much loved and respected peace officer, so it wasn't me them rubes was paid to kill."

Clayton nodded. "Yeah, you're right. Their rifles were aimed at me."

"Well, if it was Terry who hired them two, he fears you and he's willing to pay somebody else to do his killing."

Kelly placed his hand on Clayton's shoulder. "He's a dangerous man, Cage. From now on step light and"—he smiled—"stay out of dark alleys."

The marshal rose to his feet. "We'll strip the saddle and bridle off your hoss and I'll send Moses Anderson out for them. You'll have to pay him, of course."

"Are we going to bury the men you killed?"

"With what? Our bare hands? Moses will plant 'em, if he can find them."

Clayton picked up his rifle as Kelly swung into the saddle.

"Climb up behind me," the marshal said. "And try not to attract the attention of any more bushwhackers, huh?"

Chapter 37

A month passed and the summer heat grew more oppressive. Hammered by the sun, Bighorn Point was dusty, dreary, and deserted. The sawn timber of the buildings warped and smelled of beaded pine resin, and nobody went outside unless it was really necessary.

Like many another man in town, Cage Clayton gazed often on the Sans Bois and dreamed of their shadowed, ferny places where green frogs splashed in rock pools and stuck out their tongues at hovering dragonflies.

Reluctant to make any kind of physical effort, he sat in a rocker on the shaded hotel porch, too sapped to move anything but his eyes.

There had been no more attempts on Clayton's life, and Bighorn Point seemed content to quietly drowse the summer away, waiting with listless patience for the first winds of winter.

Over at the livery, Benny Hinton had tried to sell

139

Clayton a yellow mustang that must have weighed less than eight hundred pounds. The little horse had a mean eye, a swayed back, and a cough, but Hinton insisted the thirty-dollar nag was a veritable Bucephalus, ready to carry the man from Abilene on any adventure.

Clayton passed and Hinton, irritated, said he'd find him another. He didn't add, "just as bad," but Clayton reckoned it was on the tip of his tongue.

He and Emma Kelly had stepped out a few times, but, uneasy and constantly on his guard for assassins, he knew he hadn't been good company for a young girl.

He thought Emma liked him well enough, but he wasn't sure. And that was where things stood between them.

Then, the morning that Mayor Quarrels hired some loafers to water the street in an attempt to keep down the clouds of dust that coated everything in town with a layer of yellow grit, Angus McLean arrived in Bighorn Point.

And everything changed.

The little Scotsman, sour and ill-tempered, rolled into town in a dray driven by Moses Anderson. The once-a-month passenger car had arrived at the spur, and Moses had been unloading barrels of beer from the only boxcar.

The big black man had only been too glad to offer McLean a ride into town, but the two dollars he'd charged rankled the Scotsman. Now, standing beside the grinning Anderson he vented his outrage on Marshal Kelly, who had joined Clayton on the hotel porch.

"Two dollars this damned Hindoo is charging me," McLean yelled. "It's highway robbery, I tell ye."

Kelly smiled. "It's the going rate, Mr. . . . ."

"McLean. Angus McLean of Edinburgh Toon. Here to buy a ranch and cattle, no to be robbed by Hindoos."

Moses Anderson was a huge man, well over six feet with bulging muscles to match. His hair was graying at the sides, but he had the quick, amused eyes of a teenager. "It's better than walking," he said.

McLean turned on the man, cupped his hand to his mouth, and yelled, "Ye're a robber!"

"Two dollars," Anderson said, grinning, holding out a palm the size of a shovel.

McLean cursed under his breath, removed a steel purse from his pocket, and extracted a couple of coins. The purse snapped shut like a bear trap.

"Here, and be damned to ye, and you're a bandit, so ye are."

After the grinning Moses left, Kelly said, "Are you staying long in Bighorn Point, Mr. McLean?"

"I am not. Just long enough to conduct my business. I'm told you have a stage through here."

"Day after tomorrow at noon."

"Then I'll be on it."

"Have you found a ranch yet, or are you just looking?" Clayton asked.

"Oh, I've found one all right, if it stands up to my scrutiny. For the last couple of months, I've been dealing with the lassie who's selling it through my lawyers in Boston."

Suddenly Clayton was interested. "Would that be Lee Southwell?"

"Aye, it would. Do you know her?"

"We're . . . acquainted," Clayton said.

The hotel doors were opened to catch the nonexistent breeze and McLean looked past the two men into the lobby. "Weel, I'd better get my room and lay doon my bag. I can't stand this infernal heat."

Then, as though he'd just remembered something, he said to Kelly, "Is there somebody who can drive me oot to the ranch?"

The marshal nodded. "Moses Anderson has a gig. He can take you out to the Southwell spread."

"You mean the brigand that just robbed me?"

"Either him, or you can rent a horse at the livery."

"Damn it all, man, I canna ride a horse."

"Then Moses is your man," Clayton said.

A suspicious look crossed McLean's face. "Are you two in cahoots?"

"No."

"How much will he charge me?"

"I don't know," Kelly said. "You'll have to ask him."

"He'll rob me."

The marshal smiled. "Probably."

McLean's narrow shoulders slumped. "I'm going to end up in the poorhouse, so I am."

The Scotsman checked into the hotel and reappeared ten minutes later, his black frock coat just as dusty as it was when he went inside. "Where do I find that Hindoo highwayman?"

Kelly pointed the way and McLean said to Kelly, "If I'm no back by dark, come looking for me, Constable. Not that it will matter. You'll probably find me robbed of my purse and my throat cut."

Chapter 38

"If McLean's lawyers have been talking to Lee Southwell for the past couple of months, she planned to sell the ranch before her old man was even in the ground," Clayton said.

"Seems like," Kelly said.

"Maybe Southwell was murdered."

"That's a possibility."

"Probability, I'd say." Clayton looked over at Kelly on the next rocker. "How's the beer?"

"Warm."

Clayton took his own schooner from the porch rail and tried it. "Well, it's wet."

"Yeah, it is at that."

"Can you arrest Lee Southwell and Shad Vestal on suspicion of murder?"

Kelly sipped his beer. "No."

"But if she planned to sell the ranch—"

"Who's to say that it wasn't Park who wanted to sell it? Lee always talked about going east to live in Boston or New York. Park could have finally caved and agreed to her demands."

"But it was Lee who contacted McLean."

"You ever married, Cage?"

"No."

"Figured that. Married men often let their wives handle business deals. Keeps peace in the happy home. Park could have been no exception." Kelly lazily turned his head. "In other words, I'd be laughed out of court, especially when everybody knows Parker Southwell died gallantly leading a cavalry charge."

"Yeah, but Vestal could've popped him and blamed the bandits."

"He could, and I believe he probably did, but believing and proving are different things."

"So Lee and Vestal take McLean's money and run."

"Right now, that's how it's shaking out."

"And the dead Apaches?"

"I can't take that to court either. The whole town believes outlaws attacked the train at the spur, and they'll believe any lawyer who says the same

144

outlaws murdered the kidnapped Apaches." He looked at Clayton again. "You really believe a jury of eight men could look at Lee Southwell on the stand, sobbing into her little lace hankie, and find her guilty of anything?"

"Damn beer is getting warmer," Clayton said. He sighed. "No, they wouldn't find her guilty."

"Case closed," Kelly said.

A silence stretched between the two men. A Cooper's hawk glided across the blue bowl of the sky, then dove, and somewhere beyond the town a little death happened.

Dust kicking up from his feet, a dog crossed the street and vanished into an alley. A bottle clinked, marking his passing.

The last of Mayor Quarrels's watermen quit, took off his hat, and scratched his bald head. The empty street was as dry and dusty as ever, the water already evaporated.

Down at the church a woman stepped outside, applied a polishing cloth to the door brasses, then thought the better of it and went back inside.

A lizard ran along the porch rail, then stopped, its sides heaving.

Kelly watched the lizard for a while, then said, "Cage, ain't you bored with it yet?"

"Bored with what?"

"This town . . . waiting for a man to reveal himself so you can kill him."

"I'm running out of money," Clayton said.

"Maybe Lissome Terry, whoever he is now, knows that. Maybe he figures he can wait you out."

Clayton shook his head. "No, Nook, he'll make a move. He's just been lying low, biding his time."

"Well, I sure hope so. I'm getting bored all to hell again."

Irritated slightly, Clayton said, "If I got shot, would that help?"

Kelly brightened. "It sure would. Give me something to do."

Clayton decided not to fill in the silence that followed, but Kelly did it for him.

"Emma likes you," he said.

"How do you know?"

"She told me so."

"I thought I bored her like I bore you."

Kelly nodded. "Yeah, strange, that, but you don't. All she talks about is Cage. Cage said this and Cage said that and Cage—"

"I get the picture."

"Well, she likes you." Kelly turned his head. "I thought you should know."

After a while, Clayton said, "I'm too old for her. I'm used up and I'm broke. Hell, I don't even own a horse. What do I have to offer her?"

"Get a job."

"I've got a job."

"I mean a regular job. A forty-dollar-a-month job."

"Yeah, forty a month is going to keep Emma in style."

"Some married couples have done with less."

Kelly held his beer glass to the light.

"Damn, I'm sure I saw a fly in there," he said. "I guess not."

He looked at Clayton. "Cage, get married and hang that gun you're wearing on a nail. Use it to shoot coyotes."

"After my work here is done, I'll think about it."

"Think hard, because you aren't cut out to be a gunfighter. You've killed two men and crippled another, so let it go at that."

Kelly took the makings from Clayton's pocket. "You know why I'm bored, Cage?"

"Because nobody's killed me yet?"

"That, and because my time is over and I know it. Most of the men I rode with back in the old days are dead or in jail. America doesn't need gunfighters anymore. She needs engineers, road builders, factory workers, men to plow the land. Fellas like me are going—what's the word?— extinct." Kelly smiled. "I walk around this town with its church and school like yesterday's ghost. My gun skills are in such high demand, Mayor Quarrels pays me two bits a head to shoot stray dogs."

Kelly's chair creaked as he shifted his weight. "I'm hauling my freight, Cage. The French are paying big money for laboring men to help dig a canal down Panama way, and there's talk our own government will soon get involved."

"Nook, I can't see you using a shovel and swinging a pick," Clayton said.

"Maybe not, but I'm going to give it a try."

Kelly finally lit his cigarette. "You ever think that Lissome Terry might be dead?" he said.

"He's not."

"How do you know? All men die, some sooner than others."

"He's here, in Bighorn Point. I can feel him, smell his stink."

Kelly's breath sighed through his chest like a forlorn breeze. "Cage, marry Emma. Build a new life for yourself."

Chapter 39

The day was shading into evening when Angus McLean returned to Bighorn Point.

Moses Anderson dropped him off at the hotel where Clayton and Kelly still sat on the porch, content, for this day at least, to let the world go on without them.

To Clayton's surprise, McLean staggered a little as he stepped down from the gig; then he saw the reason. Moses tilted back his head and drained the last drop from a whiskey bottle before tossing it into the street.

McLean looked at the black man and made a small, unsteady bow.

"A robbing Hindoo ye may be," he said, "but you're a bonnie lad and you've done me a great service this day." The little Scotsman hiccupped. "If you're ever in Edinburgh, pay me a visit and I'll give ye the best my poor hoose has to offer."

He turned and, with that stiff-kneed dignity possessed by only the truly drunk, negotiated the two steps to the porch.

"Well, Mr. McLean," Kelly said, "do you own a ranch?"

"That I do, Constable," McLean said. "The lassie drove a hard bargain and the land and cattle cost me a lot of silver, but the bargain was made and the deed was done and there's an end to it."

He waved a hand, unsteadying himself, and Kelly rose quickly and helped him remain on his feet.

"Thank ye, Constable. Thank ye kindly." The Scotsman waved his hand again. "Yon black laddie is a robber through and through, but he knows the land and he knows cattle and he taught me much."

McLean hiccupped again. "I mean, aboot the grass and the water and the coos. And another thing, he can stand his whiskey like a man. Like a Scotsman, if I'm no mistaken."

Smiling, Kelly said. "Moses has been up the trail a few times. He knows cattle and grass."

McLean nodded. "That he does. Benighted Hindoo he may be, but he's a clever lad."

"When will you move onto the Southwell Ranch, Mr. McLean?" Kelly said.

McLean reared back as though he'd been slapped. "Never, I say! My home is in Edinburgh in bonnie Scotland. No, laddie, this wilderness of dust and drought is not for Angus McLean." He tapped the side of his nose with a long forefinger. "I'll hire a manager. He'll run the place for me."

"Do you have one in mind?"

"No, not in mind. But my lawyers in Boston will find a likely lad. I'm sure of that."

"There's a likely lad right here, Mr. McLean. This is Mr. Cage Clayton and he owned his own ranch at one time. Now he's looking for work."

Before Clayton could object, Kelly said, "And he's getting married soon."

"Is that right?" McLean said. He looked at Clayton like a molting owl. "What happened to your own ranch?"

"Three years of drought and poor cattle prices," Clayton said. "But I'm not looking for a job."

"Do ye know coos and grass and water?"

"Yes, I do, and a lot more besides. But, as I told you, I don't need a job."

"And getting wed too." McLean shook his head. "Ah, weel, you're a fine young man and you look a person in the eye, and that's all to the good. So, if you change your mind . . ."

150

"I won't."

McLean nodded. "It's me for my bed. The drive out to the ranch and the bargaining has fair wore me out." He lifted his hat. "Good night to ye both, gentlemen."

After McLean was gone, Kelly said, "Marry Emma and take the ranch manager's job. Settle down, Cage, and forget Lissome Terry."

Clayton smiled. "Maybe I'd consider it if I thought for one moment that Terry's forgotten me."

Chapter 40

"Think of it, Shad. We can go east—Boston, New York, even Europe. All the wonderful places I've only dreamed about," Lee Southwell said.

"Until the money runs out," Vestal said. "What then?"

"I don't care. By then we'll have lived, Shad, lived my dream. And you by my side, sharing it with me."

Vestal smiled. "Don't worry. I'll have thought of a way to make money by the time ol' Park's dough is spent."

Lee put her hand on his arm. "Of course you will, my darling."

"Before we leave, I have a little job to do for the Hog."

The woman was alarmed. "Not me, Shad. Please say it's not me."

"No, it's not you."

A shudder shivered through her and she pulled her shawl closer. "I couldn't bear that sweating pig grunting on top of me again."

"He paid us well enough." Vestal smiled. "We'll spend his money in Paris."

Lee lifted her beautiful eyes to Vestal's face. "It was worth it, Shad, wasn't it? All the times I let him ride me like a mare?"

"Of course it was worth it. Count the money in your dresser drawer if you need convincing."

"You don't mind? I mean, that I was with him for so long?"

Vestal shook his head. "No, I don't mind. It was only business, just like gunning Park was business."

The moonlight caught in Lee's hair and cast one side of her face in shadow. "I thought Parker would never die," she said.

"Me too. That's why I helped him along. He rode my bullet into hell."

The woman laid her head on Vestal's chest. "You're so good to me, Shad, and I love you so much."

"You proved that today, Lee. You proved that when you told the Scotsman that we were the co-owners of the ranch."

The woman smiled, her mouth still close to Vestal's chest. "You suppose his check is good?"

"It's good all right. That little man still has the

first penny he ever earned." Vestal grinned, his voice affecting McLean's accent. "Dealing with you two rrrobbers will put me in the poorrr-house."

Lee drew her head back and laughed. "Let's go back to the house, darling, and make some plans."

"No, it's nice out tonight. Let's walk some more."

"I'm getting tired, so only to the cottonwood and back." She smiled at Vestal. "Where will we go first? Boston? New York? Or should we spend a few weeks in Denver before heading east?"

Vestal smiled. "Well, Lee, I can't answer that because we have a problem."

The woman stopped walking and showed alarm again. "What sort of problem?"

"The Hog wants me to kill Cage Clayton first."

Lee sighed her relief. "Oh, for a moment there, I thought it was something serious."

"Killing a friend of Kelly's could be serious."

"You can take care of Kelly."

"Sure I can."

"Then there is no problem."

They stood under the cottonwood, the moon bright enough to cast skeletal fingers of shadow on the grass. The wind was rising, blowing a tendril of hair across Lee's forehead.

"We have a bigger problem," Vestal said.

Lee looked up at him and smiled. "Shad, now

you're just being silly. You're teasing me, aren't you?"

Vestal shook his head. "When I was a boy, my ma didn't stick around for long, but before she left she taught me how to read and do my ciphers."

Lee's perplexed face asked the question that Vestal now answered.

"I can add, subtract, and divide real well. After the Scotsman left, I added up the money for the ranch, the money we saved, and what I'll get for killing Clayton."

His voice like death, he said, "Then I divided by two."

Lee shrank from him, her back bumping against the trunk of the cottonwood.

"Shad," she said, her words trembling, "what are you saying?"

"I'm saying that there's only enough money for one person—me."

"But I love you, Shad. We'll make the money last. We'll be happy."

"Sorry, Lee. It just wouldn't work out."

Vestal slid a carving knife from his waistband and in one fast, fluid motion, rammed it into the woman's chest to the hilt, just below her left breast. She slid down the tree trunk, her eyes on him, a mix of disbelief and horror. Blood stained the front of her white dress like a scarlet heart.

"Why . . . how . . . how could you . . . Shad . . ."

"It's only business," Vestal said. "Nothing personal."

But he was talking to a dead woman, and out among the shadowed hills the coyotes were already singing Lee Southwell's desolate elegy.

Chapter 41

The lone rider sat his paint among the shadows cast by the moon glow upon the pines. He'd watched the Hunter and the woman for a long time before the man pulled his knife and killed her.

When he saw the flash of moonlight on the blade, and heard it plunge home, the rider grunted deep in his chest. The woman meant nothing to him, but the thought came to him again that the Hunter was a dangerous and ruthless enemy. To kill a woman was to kill without honor, but the Hunter's heart was bad and he did not care.

The rider had thought about shooting at him with his rifle, but the light was uncertain and he was old and his hands shook. He would have missed. He knew that. After the Hunter left, the old man rode down the slope to the cottonwood where the woman sprawled in death, her eyes open.

She was pretty in the face and body and could have borne many sons.

Aaaiii, it was a waste.

Lamps were lit in the Hunter's house, but the old man could not see him. No matter, he would not try to kill him now.

He spat in the direction of the ranch house, his eyes ablaze with black fire.

The Hunter's time would come.

Soon. Before the next dawn.

Chapter 42

Cage Clayton woke to the hammering on his door. He slid the Colt from the holster hanging from the bedpost and said, "Who is it?"

"It's me, Emma."

It took a few moments for the significance of that to penetrate Clayton's sleep-fuddled brain, and finally he said, "I'm not decent."

The girl silvered a laugh. "Then get decent. I'll wait for you in the lobby."

"Why?" Clayton cursed under his breath. *A pretty girl at my hotel room door and all I can say is "Why?"*

"You're taking me to breakfast," Emma said. "And I don't have much time before I start work."

Clayton swung his legs off the bed and put on his hat. "I'll be right down."

"Don't be too long."

He found one sock, but couldn't locate the other, and when he slipped his canvas suspenders over his shoulders, he discovered that he'd buttoned up his shirt wrong. His left boot pulled on just fine, but the other stuck on his heel, then twisted, and he had to start all over again.

Clayton wet down his hair, ran a comb through it, and wished he'd had time to trim his mustache. When he glanced in the mirror, he wasn't pleased by what he saw—a man with age lines in his face, wearing scuffed down-at-heel boots and a shirt and pants that had faded to no color at all. Thank goodness his hat looked fine, a new gray Stetson that had cost him a month's wages.

Clayton had seen enough. He opened the door and walked downstairs to the lobby.

Emma Kelly took his breath away. She wore a pink gingham dress, ribbons of the same color in her hair. She was as fresh and pretty as a May morning, stepping into the day clean, like sunlight.

Suddenly, Clayton felt big and awkward, all hands and feet, shabby in his clothes, fumbling for words like a man sorting through a pile of rags.

"You look real pretty, Miz Emma," he said finally.

"And you are as handsome as ever, Mr. Clayton." The girl smiled.

Again Clayton drew back, baffled by her praise.

Emma saved him. "Will you give me your arm?"

"Yes," he said. It was the only word he could find.

The restaurant was busy so early in the morning, and Ma poured them coffee while they waited on their orders.

Emma's smile was bright. "So, I hear you were offered a job," she said.

"You've been talking to Nook," Clayton said.

"Ranch manager," Emma said. "You're coming up in the world."

"I wasn't offered the job. Nook volunteered me for it."

"He says it's yours if you want it."

"Nook talks too much."

"Well, is it?"

"Is it what?"

"You know what I'm talking about, Cage," Emma said, her lowered brows scolding. "Is the job yours for the taking?"

"Maybe. I don't know. McLean didn't even mention what he's paying."

"You should ask him."

Clayton was silent for a while. The steamy heat of the restaurant made sweat trickle down his back. Emma on the other hand seemed unaffected by it.

"You know why I'm in Bighorn Point," he said. "I've made no secret of that."

"Nook says he thinks Lissome Terry is dead."

"I don't. I believe he's here in town. He paid a couple of grub line farm boys to kill me. Nook Kelly knows that."

"He thinks maybe he was mistaken, that the bushwhackers only wanted your horses and guns."

"Nook doesn't really believe that."

Now Clayton waded into water he knew was too deep for him. "He wants me to take McLean's job and marry you, settle down."

To his surprise, Emma took that in stride. "You could do worse, Cage Clayton," she said.

He matched Emma's honesty with his own. "Yes, I know I could. But I don't want McLean's job. At least, not yet."

When their breakfasts arrived, they ate in silence. When she was finished eating, only a few bites here and there, Emma rose to her feet.

"I must be getting to work."

Clayton dabbed his mouth with his napkin. "I'll come with you."

"No, stay and finish your food." Emma tried to smile, failed, then said, "I have some thinking to do."

When the girl reached the door, Clayton called out, "Emma, I'll talk to Angus McLean, hear what he has to say."

He didn't know if she'd heard him or not.

Chapter 43

"Eighty dollars a month, Mr. Clayton, and there's my best offer," Angus McLean said.

"I was paying my top hand that much," Clayton said.

"Aye, and look what happened to you."

"Add a twenty to the wage."

"A hundred a month? Are ye daft, man?"

"You won't find a better ranch manager, not around these parts or in Boston either."

McLean rocked back and forth on the hotel porch, nursing a hangover, his mood as sour as curdled cream.

"Ye're a robber, so ye are," he said.

"A hundred a month. I'll have a wife to support, remember."

"Marrying that lassie the constable was talking aboot?"

"If she'll have me."

The Scotsman turned and looked at Clayton. After a while he said, "Aye, weel, she might. There's no accounting for some lassies' tastes."

Again McLean lapsed into silence; then, "Ninety dollars a month, and another ten if ye prove to be satisfactory after a calendar year."

The Scotsman's eyes hardened. "I'll only accept

your best work, mind. If ye shirk your duties, then out ye go."

"Agreed."

McLean leaned out of his rocker. "Then here's my hand on it. You're hired. You'll be hearing from my lawyers who'll draw up a contract."

"I appreciate it, Mr. McLean," Clayton said.

"Your best work. I want that ranch to make a profit."

"It will."

"Aye, weel, I'll take you at your word."

McLean's eyes drifted down the street where shadows angled in the morning sun. "Ah, here's Moses coming. He's taking me out to see more of the range I just bought. Sharp as a tack, that laddie."

When Anderson stopped the rig at the porch, McLean yelled, "Did you bring a bottle, ye damned heathen?"

The black man grinned and held up a bottle of Old Crow. "And I brung some fried chicken an' sourdough biscuits my woman cooked," Anderson said.

McLean rose to his feet. "And you'll charge me for it, nae doubt."

"No, it's all included in the price, Mr. McLean."

"Aye, and the price is high enough as it is, I'll be bound. Ye're a robbing Hindoo and there's the case stated plain and square."

McLean climbed into the gig, then turned to Clayton.

"I'll be back this evening and we'll talk some more," he said. "Bring the lassie with you."

"I'll do that," Clayton said.

But would Emma agree to come?

Chapter 44

Shad Vestal ignored the whiskey bottle and drank coffee. A man who planned to murder six human beings had to stay sober.

He sat in Park Southwell's favorite leather chair, in a parlor with female touches that should have reminded him of Lee. It didn't. The whore was gone. He would soon have her money, so why even think about her?

Women came cheap and he'd have his fill of them. *Glutted.* He'd heard Park use that word once and it had tickled him ever since. He'd have so many women he'd be glutted.

"Glut-ted," he said aloud. The sound of the word pleased Vestal and he smiled.

"Hello the house!"

Vestal stiffened. Not the law, not Kelly. A voice he didn't recognize.

He rose to his feet, lifted a Colt from the table, and tucked it behind him into his waistband. He opened the door.

"Hell, it's you, Moses," he said.

The black man moved forward in his seat. "And Mr. McLean."

A sudden surge of panic spiked Vestal. Had the little Scotsman changed his mind?

"Just passing by, Mr. Vestal," McLean said. "Taking another look at the range and the cattle and buildings appertaining thereto."

Relieved, Vestal said, "Then step down and have a drink."

McLean held up a skinny hand. "Oh, dearie me, no. I don't want to intrude; just driving past." He looked around him. "And where is the bonnie lassie?"

"She's out riding," Vestal said. "I'm surprised you didn't meet her."

"Well, we might see her on the way back."

Vestal stepped beside the gig. "When are you headed back to Boston, Mr. McLean?"

"Tomorrow on the noon stage. After that I'll make my train connections."

The Scotsman studied Vestal's face. "You're not worried about the check, are ye?"

Vestal affected a smile. "Of course not. But I've decided to come with you to Boston."

"Ye have? Why in the world would you want to do that?"

"Lee and I talked it over. We agreed that I should leave her here to get her affairs in order, then meet her in Boston." Vestal shook his head. "You know what strange notions women get."

"No, I do not," McLean said, "since I never saw the need to enter a state of wedlock." He thought for a few moments, then said, "Ach, weel, you'll be company on the journey." His face grew crafty. "But you'll pay your own way, mind."

"Of course."

"Then I'll see you the morn at the stage. Don't be late, now. I won't hold it for you."

Vestal nodded. "Don't worry. I'll be there."

"I'm off, then," McLean said. "I'll say good day to ye."

After he watched the rig vanish from sight behind a billow of dust, Vestal walked back into the house.

Things were shaping up perfectly. He'd forget about the Hog's contract to gun Clayton. With no time to plan, Nook Kelly, a born meddler, could make the job too dangerous.

He closed the door quietly behind him, smiling.

Now he had men to kill. And that he had planned.

Vestal had called the ranch's six surviving hands off the range. Now that the place was sold and the servants dismissed, the men were on edge, concerned about their futures. In the changing West, gun wages were hard to come by and jobs were scarce for those who knew only the way of the Colt.

Vestal, smiling, reassuring, stepped into the

bunkhouse, and tried to set the hands' minds at rest.

Every single one of them would be well taken care of, he told them. Mr. Southwell in his will had left each man a year's wages in the event of his death.

A lie. He had left everything to Lee.

He, Vestal, would try to find any man who wanted one a job, though he had heard—and don't spread this around—that Angus McLean was interested in keeping gun hands on the payroll.

"See, you've got nothing to fear, boys," Vestal said, beaming. "Why, old Park's death could end up being the best damn thing that ever happened to you."

A hollow cheer went up from the men, followed by a second, louder one when Vestal said, "Come up to the house, boys. Park had the best cellar in the territory and tonight I want to see you drink it dry."

"Any whores, Shad?" a man yelled.

"No, Lee is spending the night in town," Vestal said.

That last caused a bellow of laughter and Vestal joined in the mirth. Or seemed to. Inwardly he felt only a sense of triumph.

Yes, laugh now, you sorry trash. By the time the sun comes up tomorrow, you'll be humping the Devil's whores in hell.

Chapter 45

Men who hug the bottle too closely get drunk and noisy, then quiet and maudlin, and finally, and mercifully, they fall into a coma that's a mean approximation of sleep.

It took the Southwell hands five hours to complete the process, just as the day slipped into night.

Vestal pretended to drink, sipping slowly and little. He joined in the laughter, the reminiscences, shed crocodile tears when they sang "She's More to Be Pitied Than Censured," and he watched with growing anticipation as heads drooped and men sprawled across the bottle-littered dining table and snored.

Later Vestal would tell himself that it was all sinfully easy, so easy that he reckoned years from now the memory of it would make him smile.

There was no fuss, no bother.

He fetched a carving knife from the kitchen and, one by one, cut six throats.

Oh, sure, a couple bubbled blood and one cried out, but the job was done quickly and Vestal was more than satisfied.

He walked to the kitchen, stripped off his bloody clothes, then scrubbed his hands and body with soap and water. He stepped into Park's bedroom, found pants, slippers, and a smoking jacket he liked, and put them on.

Vestal returned to the dining room, where he sat at the top of the table, old Park's place.

He poured himself a brandy, nodding his appreciation as he savored its musky, fruity aroma and taste.

The earth and its pleasures are for the living, not the dead.

It dawned on Vestal then, as it had many times in the past, that the dead are quiet. They hear nothing and spread no tales.

He lit a cigar, one of Park's slim Havanas.

The hands had to die, of course.

They knew too much. All of them had culled Apaches, and alive could point fingers, tell tales.

Vestal nodded and aloud he said, "You're in a better place now, boys."

And that made him laugh. He splashed more brandy into his glass.

Later, he packed a single carpetbag. He could buy clothes in the latest style in Boston or wherever. He laid his holstered Colt at the bottom of the bag. He wouldn't need it now. Later perhaps, but for the moment he wished to project an image of the rich, successful gentleman.

With that in mind, he went to his room and laid out his best go-to-prayer-meeting suit, white shirt, new elastic-sided boots, and then, his crowning glory, a cream-colored bowler hat, made in England of the finest felt.

He'd never worn these clothes before, but had bought them as part of his long-range plans.

Vestal looked in the mirror and admired the outrageously handsome man who stared back at him. Yellow hair cascaded in waves to his shoulders, his eyes were of the clearest blue, and his mustache was full, flowing, and magnificent.

That last would make the hearts of many a Boston belle flutter, he knew.

Perhaps he'd marry one, for her money of course. And then . . . well, he still had his gun.

Women were such useful but wonderfully disposable commodities.

As he had done with Lee, Vestal decided to leave the bodies where they lay. By the time anyone came out this way, he'd be long gone.

But now the silent dead bored him.

He lit another cigar, poured more brandy, and stepped outside into the cool of the evening.

The stars looked so close, Vestal believed he could reach out and grab a handful, then scatter them on the ground and let them burn out until only cinders were left.

Somewhere in the gloom the coyotes were calling close and a night bird—

Suddenly Vestal was alert.

He had never heard a bird call like that on the Southwell range.

There it was again, a soft warble. A short spell of quiet; then it was repeated.

Instinctively he reached for his gun. No! He'd left it in the carpetbag.

The Apaches came at him in a rush.

Chapter 46

To Cage Clayton's joy, Emma agreed to meet him on the hotel porch after she finished work. At the appointed time, she showed up on the arm of Nook Kelly, who arrived grim-faced and silent.

"I'm meeting Angus McLean this evening," Clayton said. He looked at Emma. "He wanted you to be here."

The girl smiled, but it was a wan effort. "Cage, I can't talk you into taking his job. That's a decision only you can make for yourself."

"I took the job," Clayton said. "Ninety a month, and another ten after a year." Now he plunged in again. "We can live on that."

Emma made no answer, and Clayton said, "Can't we?"

She rushed into his arms. "Of course we can! Oh, Cage, this is wonderful news."

Kelly stuck out his hand. "Congratulations. You'll do a terrific job."

Clayton shook hands, but his eyes never left Kelly's.

"He's still alive, you know," he said. "Despite what you told Emma, Lissome Terry is in Bighorn Point."

He watched the lawman struggle with the lie that hovered on the tip of his tongue, but in the end the truth clenched out of him.

"Yes, he . . . probably is."

Emma swung her head. "But, Nook, you said that Terry—"

"Was dead? I told you that because I thought you might be able to convince Cage it was the truth."

He looked at Clayton. "Enjoy the new job, Cage. Leave Terry to me."

"He'll get tired of waiting, of looking over his shoulder," Clayton said. "And eventually he'll come after me."

"If he does that, I'll be ready."

Clayton shook his head. "No, I'll be ready. This is my fight, not yours."

"I'm the law in this town and that makes it my fight."

"Oh, for heaven's sake, I can't bear to hear you two squabbling over which of you gets to kill a man," Emma said. "Can't you forget about Terry, let his own guilty conscience make him suffer?"

"I don't think he has one of those," Clayton said.

Emma stared at Clayton. "Cage, do you want to marry me?"

"Of course I do."

"Then forget that terrible man. Think about us."

Kelly smiled. "Sounds like good advice."

"It is good advice," Clayton said, "and I'll take it—until the time comes."

"Terry is dead," Emma said, "dead to us."

Clayton nodded, glad he had no need to add words to the gesture.

Angus McLean arrived an hour before dark. He dismissed Moses Anderson with a stern warning that he should change his robbing ways "instanter," heed the teachings of the Church of Scotland, and make sure he visited Edinburgh Town at his earliest convenience.

Moses smiled, bobbed his head, and promised to do all of the above.

"Aye, weel, I hope ye do," McLean said. He found his steel purse, opened it wide so it gaped like the jaws of a shark, and extracted some coins.

"Here, a wee bonus to ye for your help," he said. "Don't spend it on whiskey and scarlet women, mind."

He thought about that; then, "Weel, the whiskey is all right, but stay away from the painted Jezebels."

"Praise the Lord," Moses said, grinning.

"You're learning," McLean said. "Now be off with ye, and damn ye for a thieving Hindoo."

The Scotsman watched Moses leave, then

turned to Kelly and said, "A lad o' parts, that one. He'll go far and make his mark or my name's not Angus McLean." He looked at Emma. "And this is the lassie who'll be taking care of my ranch house and all the outbuildings pertaining thereto."

A thought occurred to him. "Oh, I hope I'm not speaking out of turn. Has your intended told you he's my new manager?"

"He has," Emma said, "and I want to thank you for such a wonderful opportunity." She glanced at Clayton. "And so does Cage."

McLean held up a hand. "No need for thanks, lassie. Your man is a robber, but I think he'll do well."

He smiled. "Here, Miss Southwell is still at the ranch. You should go out there and talk to her. She can show you the workings of the stove and where the washtub is kept and the scrubbers and buckets for the floor. Women stuff like that."

Kelly smiled. "I doubt that Lee Southwell has scrubbed a floor in her life."

"Aye, you may be right. She's a bonnie lassie and no mistake but not a housewife. Still, I wish it was her accompanying me to Boston and not her partner."

"Partner?" Kelly said, surprised.

"Mr. Vestal. He's a braw-looking lad, but not my cup o' tea, if you take my meaning. But he's Mrs. Southwell's partner in the ranch and I had to deal with him."

"Vestal is going with you to Boston?" Kelly said.

"Aye, we leave on the noon stage tomorrow."

"Did you talk to Lee?"

"No, I didn't see her when I stopped by the hoose earlier today. Mr. Vestal says she's staying on at the ranch for a week or so to get her affairs in order. Her being a widow woman, I suppose that's understandable."

Kelly turned to Clayton, his expression asking a question.

"She makes Vestal her partner in the ranch," Clayton said, "then lets him gallivant off to Boston without her?" He shook his head. "Doesn't sound like the Lee Southwell I know."

"No, she'd go to Boston herself and let Shad Vestal settle her affairs in Bighorn Point," Emma said. "It does seem strange."

Kelly thought about that for a while, then said, "I'll ride out there at first light, see what's on Lee's mind."

"I'm still your deputy," Clayton said. "Mind if I tag along?"

"You're welcome," Kelly said. Then, as a second thought, "Wear your gun."

Chapter 47

For the first time in his life, Shad Vestal knew fear. Big and strong, he fought frantically, but the Apaches were too many and too determined. They dragged him away from the ranch house and in the direction of the cottonwood where he had killed Lee.

The woman's body was still there where he'd left it, her face an eerie shade of purple in the gloom, black shadows in the hollows of her eyes and under her cheekbones.

Lee's eyes were wide open, staring at Vestal, and there seemed to be a slight smile on her bloodless lips.

Vestal felt like screaming.

But he didn't. Not yet. The screams would come later.

The Apaches were stripping off his clothes! He kicked out and his right boot cracked hard against a man's jaw. The Indian went down and Vestal tried to struggle to his feet.

A rifle butt rammed into his throat and he dropped to his knees. He bent over, gagging, retching up green bile.

Again he was thrown on his back and his clothes were cut off his body, leaving him shivering and naked on the grass.

The silence of the Apaches unnerved him. There

was no talk among them, no threats directed at him, just six men quietly getting on with their work.

But what work?

Vestal was dragged to his feet.

And then he knew.

A small, hot fire had been lit under a low branch of the cottonwood, its embers glowing red. Beside it, one of the Apaches held ropes.

Vestal roared his rage and fear, tried to kick out at the men around him.

But they held him, held him on his belly while a rope was tied around his hands and then his ankles.

"Money!" Vestal screamed. "I've got money and it's yours. Whiskey. Anything you want. Just let me loose."

The Apaches rolled him on his back.

He looked up, into the hard black eyes of men who did not understand the concept of mercy, but expected a man to die well.

The Hunter was not dying well.

Shad Vestal was hung from the cottonwood by his heels, his head a few inches above the fire. His beautiful hair, his pride, fell over his face and burned, turned black and crisp to the roots, charring his scalp. His sweeping dragoon mustache melted into his face. His eyebrows burned away.

He screamed; then his screams became shrieks and his shrieks became screeches and his screeches became wails.

The Apaches sat in a circle around Vestal, feeding the fire a stick at a time.

The Hunter, who had killed so many of their people, was dying like a woman and this made them deeply ashamed for him.

There are times when fire extends a small mercy. Vestal's skull could have cracked open, spilling his brains into the coals. He would have died quickly then.

But, as the wind rose and the coyotes called close, attracted by the smell of burning hair and flesh, no such mercy was given.

Vestal suffered for each searing second of his appointed hours, babbling nonsense at the end as his brain baked.

Only when dawn stained the day with light did he die. And then, as one, the Apaches rose and walked away from him.

Chapter 48

Kelly and Clayton rode out of Bighorn Point at daybreak.

Clayton rode a rented horse, a big-boned bay with a rough trot and a mouth like iron. For Clayton, the horse's gait was unfortunate because Benny Hinton had poured them coffee for the trail and most of Clayton's ended up down his shirtfront.

Kelly, who handled the tin cup without any difficulty, looked at Clayton and grinned. "Having trouble there, Cage?"

"Old coot filled the cup too full," Clayton said. "Did it on purpose too."

"Well, well, we're a tad grouchy in the morning, ain't we?" Kelly said.

"Yeah, so don't say anything nice to me or I'll shoot you right off'n that damned hoss."

Kelly laughed. "Now, that ain't likely, is it?"

"What? The sayin' or the shootin'?"

"Both, I reckon."

Ahead of them the peaks of the Sans Bois sawed into a scarlet sky and the air came at them clean and clear, scented with pine and grass and the vanilla fragrance of the new-borning day.

Clayton gave up on his coffee, threw out what was left, and made to throw the cup away.

"Give me that," Kelly said, holding out his hand. "Benny will charge us two bits if we lose one."

As the lawman leaned back and shoved the cup into his saddlebag, Clayton said, "Why does Hinton dislike me so much?"

Kelly considered that. "Maybe it's the way you look at a man," he said finally. "It's like, well, it's like you look right inside him to see what makes him what he is."

"I wasn't aware of that."

"Well, you do it. I knew a man like that once, feller by the name of John Wesley Hardin. Heard of him?"

Clayton nodded. "Yeah, gunfighter from down Gonzalez County way in Texas. Last I was told he was in prison someplace."

"He's doing twenty-five years in Huntsville, which he don't deserve. Anyway, Wes was like you. He'd stare right into a man's soul."

"So, what does Hinton have to hide that I make him so uncomfortable?"

"Nothing that I know of, unless it's his cooking. You spook a man, is all, looking at him like that. And what a man doesn't understand, he fears."

Clayton smiled. "And do I spook you, Nook?"

"No, you don't. Ol' Wes used to stare at me like that all the time over the rim of a whiskey glass, so maybe I got used to it."

"Well, I'm going to stop looking at folks that way," Clayton said.

"Ain't gonna happen, Cage. It's a thing you're born with and it won't ever go away."

"Hello the house!"

Kelly sat his horse and scanned the building. Windows stared back at him with empty eyes, the blood-streaked sky caught in their panes.

"Nobody to home," Clayton said.

"You check the bunkhouse?"

"The hands aren't there. It's like they picked up and left in a hurry."

Kelly stepped from the saddle. "We'll go inside. I'm feeling something I don't like."

Guns drawn, Clayton and Kelly entered the ranch house. There was no sound, only the tick of the grandfather clock in the hallway and a persistent, droning buzz.

They checked a couple of bedrooms, then the parlor. Everything was as it should be.

The buzz stayed with them, growing in intensity.

"Bees in the walls?" Kelly said.

Clayton lifted his shoulders. "I don't know. Could be, I guess."

A second hallway met the first, forming a T. They turned right and stepped into the room at the end of the corridor.

Shad Vestal's fancy duds were still spread out on the bed.

"All ready for his trip, huh?" Clayton said.

"Seems like," Kelly said. "But where the hell is he? And where's Lee?"

Clayton checked another room, then stepped through the dining room door after Kelly.

They walked into a charnel house.

Chapter 49

Five men were sprawled across the dining room table and another lay on the floor. Their faces were covered in a buzzing mass of fat flies, black masks that concealed the contorted features of the dead.

The room smelled sweet, of decay, and the tick of the hall clock was loud, already measuring the minutes and hours of eternity.

His stomach an uncertain thing, Clayton left the room and stepped into the kitchen, expecting to find . . . he didn't know what.

"White men don't kill like that."

Clayton turned. Kelly was framed in the doorway.

"This is Apache work," the lawman said.

"Caught the hands while they were sleeping off a drunk, you think?"

"Looks that way."

"Then where is Vestal?"

Kelly shook his head, said nothing.

Clayton made a quick search of the kitchen and discovered a heap of bloodstained clothes that had been kicked into a corner.

He picked them up and laid them out on the kitchen table.

"Expensive duds for an Apache," he said.

Kelly picked up Vestal's shirt, studied it, frowning as his mind worked.

The kitchen sink still bore pink streaks of blood, as did a carving knife that lay on the floor where it had been carelessly tossed away.

"Whoever killed those men took time to strip off his bloody clothes and wash his hands," Clayton said. "I never knew Apaches to be that dainty."

"Then how did it come up?" Kelly hesitated only a heartbeat. "In your expert opinion."

Clayton let the barb pass. "Could be that Vestal invited the hands here to celebrate his departure for Boston, got them drunk, then cut their throats."

"Why?"

"Because they knew too much about the business of killing Apaches and the sale of their bodies."

Kelly seemed to consider that, but his eyes were steel-hard, a man who intended to go his own way, no matter what. "Vestal was a gunfighter, maybe the best there was around after me. Why didn't he shoot them?"

Clayton smiled. "Think about it, Nook. A gunshot in an enclosed room is loud. Even men dead drunk can wake and go for their revolvers."

As Kelly had done earlier, he picked up the bloody shirt.

"Vestal wanted the men dead in the quickest, easiest way possible. That's why he used a knife and not a gun."

The marshal's speech slowed, as though he was talking to a child or an obvious dimwit.

"Cage, I told you, white men don't kill like that."

Clayton opened his mouth to object, but Kelly raised a hand.

"Listen to me. You're right. The hands were drunk, and so was Vestal. The Apaches found them that way, cut their throats, but took Vestal away for special treatment. He was the one they hated most and his death would be a lot slower."

"Look at the bloody clothes, the stains in the sink and on the knife," Clayton said.

"So the Apaches roughed Vestal up some, maybe cut him. They stripped him naked because that's one of the ways an Indian shows his contempt for an enemy."

"Then where is he? And where is Lee Southwell?"

"We're going to find them. I don't think they're far."

"You reckon they're still on the ranch?"

"Yeah, I do. What's left of them."

Chapter 50

Kelly was a tracker, a skill Clayton did not possess. He stood outside the door where Vestal had been taken and pointed to the footprints.

"I count five men, a couple of them wearing moccasins, the others shoes or boots." He showed a pair of parallel gouges in the dirt. "That's where Vestal's toes dragged across the ground as they hauled him away."

"And Lee?"

"You can see the tracks of a woman's high-heeled boots"—he pointed—"there and there. My guess is they let her walk to wherever they raped and murdered her."

Clayton, a man who had a live-and-let-live attitude toward Apaches, and Indians in general, had met prejudice before. Now he accepted it from Kelly as the words of a man living in his place and time.

"Let's go find them," he said.

But he didn't want to find Lee Southwell.

"Still think Shad Vestal killed those men?"

Kelly, his face like stone, drew his knife and cut the rope that held Vestal's body. The body thumped to the ground. The head, burned black to the white bone of the skull, raised a cloud of gray ashes when it hit the dying fire.

"Lee wasn't raped," Clayton said. He could think of nothing else to say.

"How do you know?" Kelly said. He was restless, his movements quick, a man on edge.

"They would've stripped her like they did Vestal."

Kelly lifted the woman's skirt and looked. "You're right. I guess they didn't."

The marshal was quiet for a while, then said, "They made her watch Vestal dying, then stabbed her." He looked at Clayton. "Whose death was the worst, his or hers?"

"There's no good death, Nook."

"Seems like."

Kelly gathered the reins of his horse.

"Mount up," he said, "we're going after them."

"Shouldn't we bury—"

"No. We're bringing in the Apaches. I'm going to hang every one of those murdering sons of bitches in the middle of the street in Bighorn Point."

Clayton hesitated. "Nook, you think that Vestal could have murdered Lee? Maybe that's the real reason he was leaving for Boston without her."

He saw it in the lawman's eyes, a strange mix of cold anger, disgust, and confusion.

"Damn it, Cage, are you a white man?"

"Yes, I guess I am."

"Then for goodness' sake start acting like one. Get up on your damned hoss and let's find those savages. They must be all tuckered out by their night's work and that means they haven't gone far."

Kelly spat. "And stop looking at me like that."

Chapter 51

The man Vestal had called the Hog was dreaming. It wasn't a pretty dream, not one of high mountain peaks and blue skies, but one of misery, cruelty, and pain. It was the kind of dream only a man like the Hog could appreciate. Lying back on his leather couch like a gigantic, sweating walrus, he smiled to himself.

Someone tapped on the door.

"What is it?" the Hog yelled, awake.

"A message from your wife, sir. She and Reverend Bates are waiting for you at the church to discuss the roof repairs."

"Who brought the message?"

"Andy Brown's boy."

"Give him a nickel and tell him to inform my wife that I'll be there in a couple of minutes."

The Hog stood and primped at his mirror, arranging his thinning hair into kiss curls on each side of his forehead. He smoothed his large mustache, adjusted his cravat and diamond stickpin, and considered himself for a moment.

Yes, he was a fine-looking man. It was no wonder that women gave him sidelong glances when he cut a dash at the church coffee socials.

But he scowled as, unbidden, a jarring thought entered his head. One woman in particular was becoming a problem. Minnie, one of the black

185

girls who worked in town, had been one of his side projects for a few weeks. She was as stupid as a rock, and might let something slip.

The Hog smiled and his reflection smiled right back. No matter, after he got rid of Clayton—the first two incompetents he'd hired for the job had failed him badly—he'd do for Minnie. He might even kill her himself. He'd enjoy that very much.

And who would suspect him of murdering a whore? That is, if anybody cared enough to investigate.

"No one," he whispered aloud to the smirking fat man in the mirror. "No one in the whole wild world."

Chapter 52

Kelly followed the Apache tracks south, five men riding unshod ponies and in no hurry to scamper back into the Sans Bois.

Clayton thought their leisurely pace indicated an absence of guilt, as far as Lee and the Southwell hands were concerned, but he said nothing, in no mood for another tongue-lashing from Kelly.

After an hour's ride through rolling country heavily forested by pine and hardwoods, they crossed Cunneo Tubby Creek, named by the Choctaw for one of their famous war chiefs.

In the shade of cottonwoods, Kelly swung down and crumbled horse dung in his fingers.

He looked at Clayton. "We're getting close."

"How do we play this, Nook?" Clayton asked.

"We ride up and arrest them."

"They'll fight."

"Maybe, maybe not. I don't know how much sand the Apaches have left."

Kelly straightened. "I reckon a mile ahead of us, no more than that."

He stepped into the saddle. "Cage, see to your weapons, revolver and rifle. I don't want a gunfight, but it may come to that."

Clayton thumbed a round into the empty chamber under the hammer of his Colt, then fed shells into his Winchester until it was fully loaded.

He turned to Kelly. "I'm ready."

The marshal smiled. "I'll say you are. Hell, for a minute there with all that artillery, you even scared me."

Kelly kneed his horse forward, but immediately drew rein.

"Cage, what I said about you not being a white man an' all don't go. You're true blue and I've never thought otherwise."

"Did we ride all this way just for you to talk pretties or to get the job done?" Clayton said.

Kelly nodded. "Just wanted you to know, is all."

After another mile, Clayton smelled smoke in the breeze.

Kelly pointed ahead of them. "There, among the trees. They've made camp."

A thin string of smoke rose above the tree canopy, tied in wispy bows by the wind.

"We . . . just ride in," Clayton said, more question than statement.

"Stay on my left," Kelly said, "and give me room. If the ball opens, it will be fast, close-up work, so go to your revolver." He looked at Clayton. "Got that?"

Clayton nodded, but said nothing.

"Then let's get 'er done," Kelly said.

They rode into the trees and the Apaches rose to their feet.

The old warrior who had taken Clayton captive stepped forward.

"You speak English?" Kelly said.

"I do," the old man said.

"Then listen up good." Kelly's eyes were never still, measuring the men opposite him, judging who was reckless enough or desperate enough to make a play. "I'm arresting you men for the murder of Lee Southwell, Shad Vestal, and six others."

He leaned forward in the saddle.

"I will escort you to Bighorn Point, see you get

a fair trial, then hang you at the mayor's convenience."

Kelly looked beyond the old man to the others. "You men, drop those rifles. Now!"

The youngest Apache was the one who was desperate enough to make the play Kelly feared.

Chapter 53

The young Apache's rifle came up as he screamed his war cry.

Suddenly Kelly's Bulldogs were in his hands and he was firing.

Clayton drew, but couldn't find a target.

Kelly, a horseback fighter, was among them, his guns hammering.

The young Apache was down, as were three others, one on his hands and knees, retching up black blood.

The old man picked up a rifle and stepped to the side, trying for a clear shot at Kelly.

"No!" Clayton yelled.

The Apache ignored him.

Clayton fired and the old man staggered. He fired again, and this time the Indian fell.

Greasy gray smoke drifted across the clearing, and Clayton's ears rang. He saw everything around him through a black tunnel, unfolding at a snail's pace, as though time had slowed down.

He saw Kelly fire at the Apache who'd dropped

to his hands and knees. The man rolled over on his side and lay still.

Thin and reedy, the badly wounded young Apache's death song rose above the silence until Kelly stopped it in midnote with a bullet.

After that, the firing ended.

The Apaches lay unmoving in death. The old man's hair looked grayer than Clayton remembered and the knuckles of his outstretched hands were misshapen and gnarled and must have pained him in life.

As he watched Kelly reload his revolvers, Clayton tried to build a cigarette. The paper shredded in his trembling fingers and the tobacco blew away.

The marshal rode beside him, took the makings from Clayton's shivering hands, and rolled the smoke. He licked the paper tube closed, put it in Clayton's mouth, and thumbed a match into flame.

"You did good, Cage," Kelly said. "Shot that damned Apache off my back."

Clayton inhaled smoke deeply. "You saw that?"

"It pays a man to see everything that's happening in a gunfight."

"Are they all dead?"

"Dead as they're ever gonna be."

"I didn't want to kill the old man."

Kelly smiled. "Well, don't let it trouble you. An

old man can kill you deader'n hell, as surely as a young one can."

"Nook, I still don't think the Apaches killed Lee and the Southwell hands. It was Vestal."

"Well, it don't matter a hill of beans now, does it?"

"We might have killed innocent men."

"You think Shad hoisted himself up over a slow fire and boiled his own brains?"

"No. The Apaches did that. It was payback time."

"Then they were guilty of murder."

Clayton's eyes roved around the dead men. "And they sure paid for it."

Kelly nodded. "That's the law. Commit murder and you pay for it."

He looked at Clayton with blue, untroubled eyes, as though a brush with danger and the deaths of six men meant nothing to him. "Finish your smoke, then help me load them Apaches onto their ponies."

He read the question on Clayton's face and said, "Cage, the citizens of Bighorn Point pay me to administer the law, but the law has to be seen to be done. They don't want my word for it. They expect to inspect the evidence."

He smiled. "You understand that, don't you?"

"Five dead Apaches is quite a haul, for Bighorn Point or anywhere else."

"Yeah, the taxpayers are gonna be real pleased."

• • •

And they were. Brass band pleased.

The town had another hero to add to their list, right up there with the gallant Colonel Parker Southwell and his band of lionhearts.

The Apaches, as wicked and treacherous as ever, had obviously been in league with the bandits the colonel had destroyed. They had taken out their murderous rage on the Southwell Ranch, killing, raping. . . .

Oh, and poor Mrs. Southwell.

That very flower of American womanhood had been outraged, then horribly murdered, her ranch *segundo*, the brave Shad Vestal, tortured and killed within her sight.

"The only fly in our ointment of valor," said Mayor Quarrels, "is that the savages were not taken alive. It would have been my great pleasure to hang them all."

Quarrels said this at the commencement of a street meeting, when Marshal Kelly was presented with a handsome gold badge made from two double eagles.

When the crowd heard the mayor talk about the hanging, they cheered wildly.

As for Clayton, being an outsider and the one who'd thrown poor Mrs. Southwell in horse piss, Mayor Quarrels only shook his hand, and a few in the crowd managed a halfhearted "Huzzah."

However, Clayton did get an invitation from

Ben St. John, the banker, to discuss his financial affairs and his forthcoming nuptials to Miss Emma Kelly.

After singling Clayton out from the crowd, the fat man pontificated on marriage and money matters.

"Marriage is a big step, Mr. Clayton, and the one way to ensure happiness is to be financially secure," he said. "As the immortal Mr. Wilkins Micawber says, 'Annual income twenty pounds, annual expenditure nineteen pounds six, result happiness. Annual income twenty pounds, annual expenditure twenty pounds ought and six, result misery.'"

St. John's eyes met Clayton's, but could not stay there, sliding away like black slugs. He looked at Clayton's chin and beamed. "Do you catch my meaning, sir?"

"Yes, I do," Clayton said.

"Then come see me at the bank. I assure you, we can put you on a path to prosperity that will enhance your marital bliss."

St. John put his hand on Clayton's shoulder. "Shall we say ten o'clock tomorrow morning?"

"I'll be there," Clayton said.

He'd disliked the man on sight, and the suspicion lingered in him that St. John might be the one.

He could be Lissome Terry.

Chapter 54

It fell to Moses Anderson to remove the bodies from the Southwell Ranch and clean up the house. He and his helpers were just finishing up when Cage Clayton rode into the yard on an inspection and swung out of the saddle.

"Bodies are all gone, Mr. Clayton," the black man said. "I took them into town earlier this morning." Anderson wiped his hands with a rag, a talking man glad of an audience. "The undertaker says they're all too far gone for him to make them pretty, so he's just gonna box 'em and bury 'em. Buryin' is tomorrow and the mayor will be there and a lot of other folks. Mayor's laid on a barrel of beer for the wake an' a hog on a spit and it's shapin' up to be a shindig. Yes, sir, a real hootenanny. "

He shrugged. " 'Course, black folks ain't invited."

Clayton smiled. "Neither am I."

"Well, Mr. Clayton, that's a real shame, an' after the way you killed them Apaches an' all."

There was an expectant look on Anderson's face, but Clayton didn't want to dwell on the subject.

"You get all the blood out of the house, Moses?"

"Sure did. She's as clean as a whistle."

Clayton waited awhile, then eased into his questions.

"Moses, you've lived in Bighorn Point for a long time, huh?"

"Sure have. Man and boy, I bin there, 'cept I went up the trail a couple of times."

"How well do you know Ben St. John?"

Clayton watched as shutters closed in Anderson's eyes.

"Not much. He don't like colored folks."

Clayton continued to look into Anderson's face without speaking.

Uneasy now, the black man said, "Folks here'bouts say he's a mean one. Foreclosing on people and takin' their property, thowin' them out on the street, an' all. But he goes to church and sits in a pew with him and his wife's name on a little brass plate and what he's done don't seem to trouble his conscience none."

A man standing by one of the wagons yelled, "Moses, we're all through here."

"Be right with you," Anderson said.

"St. John ever kill a man?" Clayton said.

The black man shook his head. "Not that I ever heard." He looked over at the wagons that were ready to pull out. "I gotta go now, Mr. Clayton."

"Wait, Moses. Is he faithful to his wife?"

The man stared into space. "I don't know."

"You've got something to tell me, Moses, and I

195

want to hear it. The more I learn about St. John, the better."

"You think he's the man you came to Bighorn Point to kill?"

"He could be."

Anderson took a step closer. "He's sparkin' a little black gal."

"I thought he didn't like coloreds."

"He don't. But that little black gal's got a thing between her legs he likes jus' fine."

"What's her name?"

"Minnie."

The name rang a bell. "She was Lee Southwell's maid."

"Was. That's right. Now she swamps the saloon and does some whorin' on the side. Ben St. John is her best customer, steadylike."

Clayton nodded. "He's not the man he seems to be. Like he leads a double life."

"He likes women, that's for sure, and the more of a whore she is, the better he likes her."

"How come the town knows nothing about this?"

"St. John is a secretive man. And a couple of women who bragged in the saloon about servicin' him ain't with us no more."

"He killed them?"

"All I know is, they ain't around, and that's all I'm sayin' on the subject, Mr. Clayton."

Anderson stepped away. "I got to go now. My

woman expects me back to town." He gave a white grin. "Collard greens, ham, and cawn bread for supper."

Moses Anderson waved as he led his two wagons from the front of the house.

It was the last time Cage Clayton saw him alive.

Chapter 55

After the wagons left, Clayton stepped into the ranch house and into silence.

Only a grandfather clock in the hallway made a sound, remorselessly ticking away time.

Clayton shivered. Damn clock made him think of death and Judgment Day.

Moses Anderson had done a good job. There was not a trace of blood left in the dining room or the kitchen, and he'd opened windows to clear the smell of decay. Someone, probably Anderson, had placed a vase of wildflowers in the kitchen window, and a vagrant bee buzzed around the blossoms.

The flowers did little to cheer the place.

Clayton walked to the dining room and stood beside the table. The room was oppressive, hot, weighing on him as though he were wearing a damp greatcoat. He felt eyes, watching, waiting, wondering why he was there.

And that spooked Clayton badly. The whole damned place did.

Determined to see this tour to the end, he walked into the parlor, furnished in an overly ornate style in the fashion of the time.

Above the fireplace, draped in black crepe, hung a picture of the gallant Custer. The great man stared belligerently across the room at the opposite wall where an oil painting of Lee was flanked by one of Parker Southwell, dressed in the gray and gold splendor of a Confederate colonel.

Tick . . . tick . . . tick . . .

The clock in the hall reminded Clayton that this was a house of the dead and he was not welcome here, not now, not ever.

Clayton had never lost the cowboy's superstitious fear of ha'nts and the restless dead and now it plagued him.

There was the time when one of his hands had been struck by lightning and his hat lay on the range for three years. No one would touch it or go near it, the cowboys riding a mile out of their way to avoid the thing.

Finally a great wind rose and took the hat away and everybody, including Clayton, was relieved.

He felt the same way about this house as he had the hat.

He went from room to room, smelled Lee's perfume in her bedroom, the gun oil, leather, and cigar tang of Parker's study.

Shad Vestal's clothes were still spread out, untouched, on the bed. Moses Anderson had been up the trail and he shared the cowboy's superstitions. He'd left the duds where they lay.

And that's what Clayton wanted to do with this house . . . leave it where it lay.

He returned to the parlor and poured himself a drink from a decanter that Moses hadn't cleared away, then built a smoke.

It was there, in that room, he decided that he couldn't bring Emma to this place.

Could they ever take a starlit walk along the creek and spoon under the cottonwood knowing that a man had hung head-down from one of its branches, suffering the agonies of the damned?

Could they spend a restful night in any of the bedrooms? Lee's? Parker's? Vestal's?

Could they eat a meal in a dining room that had witnessed the slaughter of six human beings?

Could they live with the shadows of people who were once vibrantly alive and were now lying cold in pine boxes in the undertaker's storeroom?

Clayton asked himself those questions, and the answer to all of them was an emphatic *no*.

He'd take Emma back to Abilene, start up his ranch again.

Angus McLean would need to find himself a new manager.

Chapter 56

Shack Mitchell was well pleased with himself.

He'd only been in Bighorn Point an hour, but in that time the contract had been agreed on, his fee paid up front, and he'd left on the trail of the mark.

That was how he liked to conduct his business. Get in, get out, and get lost.

The fat man had understood all that, since he'd once been in the man-killing profession himself.

"Call it professional courtesy," the fat man had said. "You trust me, and I trust you to get the job done. So there's no need to stand on ceremony. Just bring me Cage Clayton's head and then ride out."

But Mitchell didn't trust the fat man. He put his trust in nobody, and that's why he was so good at what he did—killing men who, for one reason or another, had proved troublesome for his clients.

His last project had been in El Paso, a crusading young lawyer who was getting too close to the monetary affairs of powerful and rich men. He'd settled that contract in three days, long for him, but his clients had understood. After all, a sandstorm had been blowing at the time.

The lawyer had been his twenty-ninth victim. This man Clayton, whoever the hell he was, would make it a nice round thirty.

Mitchell smiled. This would be easy peasy.

He scanned the ranch house with his field

glasses. He saw the mark move from room to room, exploring the place, and probably filling his pockets with whatever he could find.

Mitchell didn't blame him for that. Honesty was for idiots.

He slid forward his Spencer, parting the buffalo grass at the crest of the rise.

The rifle was a single shot in .45 caliber. Having only one round didn't trouble Mitchell; he seldom needed more. Sometimes he used his Colt on a mark because he was fast and accurate on the draw-and-shoot, though he did not boast of it.

Mitchell boasted of nothing. At fifty, he was a coldly proficient assassin and when not on assignment he lay low, stayed away from whiskey, and kept his mouth shut.

He did enjoy whores, but that was just scratching an itch. He didn't like women, didn't like men either, come to that. Didn't like anybody.

Perhaps his only virtue was patience.

He'd wait in the sun for as long as it took for Clayton to come out of the house—hours, days, weeks if necessary.

But the horse at the hitch rail told him that the man would leave sooner rather than later.

Then he'd kill him. Efficiently and without fuss.

Cage Clayton was startled. Had the gallant Custer just winked at him?

He studied the picture, but the general was

staring across the room just as before. It must have been a trick of the light, a reflection maybe.

But a reflection of what? And from where?

Clayton stepped to the side of the parlor window and moved the curtain just enough to look outside.

Nothing moved out there, not even the wind.

The open ground stretched away from his eyes for about a hundred yards, past a cattle pen, a cast-iron trough, and a small shed that probably held tools and branding irons.

The open ground gradually rose to a shallow ridge, crowned with grass, scattered wildflowers, and clumps of broom weed.

Clayton was suddenly tense. Custer hadn't winked at him.

Hell, I'm not that spooked.

It had to have been a brief flash of light that reflected on the glass.

A rifle barrel?

Maybe he was being foolish, imagining things. But there had already been one attempt on his life—could this be another?

If he ventured out to get his horse, he'd be an easy target for a hidden rifleman. He moved to the rear of the house, opened the back door, and stepped outside.

He drew his Colt, his heart pounding.

Where was the rifleman—if he even existed?

Real or not, the rifleman wouldn't make getting to his mount easy.

Chapter 57

Clayton moved to the corner of the house where he could see the cattle pens and the ridge. The stillness troubled him. As far as he could judge, the ridge was the most obvious place for a bushwhacker to hide. But he wasn't even sure about that. The ground between him and the ridge looked level, but it might have unseen dips and hollows that could conceal a rifleman.

Clayton wiped his sweaty palm on his shirt, then picked up his gun again. The day was hot, but a faint breath of wind rustled the cottonwoods by the creek and fanned his burning cheeks.

He studied the ridge again. Nothing stirred up there but the blooms of the wildflowers. The sky was denim blue and a few puffy clouds hovered over the Sans Bois. Somewhere a bird sang and he heard his horse toss its head, jangling the bit.

The day was peaceful, drowsy with insect sounds, and unthreatening.

Clayton holstered his gun. This was ridiculous. He was acting like an old maid who hears a rustle in every bush.

He stepped away from the corner—and a bullet splintered timber from the house wall behind him.

Without conscious thought, Clayton dove for the ground, rolled, and then sprinted for the cattle pens. He fetched up against a post, breathing hard, and pulled his gun.

His wounded thigh was healing, but now it pained him, an insistent throb, reminding him of his clumsy surgery back at the railroad spur.

Clayton looked quickly around the post, caught a glimpse of smoke on the ridge, then ducked back down as another bullet chipped wood near his head.

Clayton swore. Whoever the man was up there on the ridge, he was a fair hand with a rifle. Both his shots had been real close. If the bushwhacker caught him in the open, if only for a second, he was a dead man.

Shack Mitchell cursed. For some reason his damned shooting was off today. He'd fired twice at the cowboy—that's what he looked like—and missed.

This had never happened to him before and it wounded his professional pride.

He'd anticipated an easy kill and hadn't put his whole concentration into the job. Well, now he would. He wouldn't miss a third time.

The mark was pinned down at the cattle pens and he had nowhere to go. All he could do now was wait until dark and make his move.

And Mitchell would be still waiting and ready.

He was angry now, angry at himself, and as mean as a teased rattlesnake.

All right, the man called Clayton would get it in the belly.

And he'd die slow.

Mitchell smiled at the thought.

Wait . . . now what the hell was this?

The mark was on the move. *Stupid. Stupid. Stupid.*

Mitchell's smile grew into a grin as he shouldered his rifle.

Clayton considered the Southwell Ranch a bad luck spread, and now a tiny, striped kitten proved it.

The little animal stepped toward him, stopped, and looked up at his face with luminous green eyes.

"Git," Clayton said. He threw a wisp of straw at the kitten. "You scat!"

The animal ignored him, purring, as it walked soundlessly toward him.

Clayton cursed. Now the bushwhacker would know exactly where he was—the damned cat was pointing him out.

"Scat!" Clayton said again.

The kitten ran to him and jumped onto his lap, then got up on her hind legs and rubbed her forehead over his chin.

"Cat, you're gonna get us both killed," Clayton said.

The kitten purred, smiled at him, and kept on with what she was doing.

Clayton shook his head. Well, that settled it, he couldn't stay here all day and let the bushwhacker flank him or get around behind him. He lifted the kitten and set her down. He jumped to his feet, his Colt up and ready.

Clayton sprinted for the cover of the trough, firing at the ridge as he ran.

He knew he'd made a bad mistake when he heard the flat hammer of gunshots. He dove for the shelter of the shed, his right shoulder coming up hard against its weathered timber.

To his surprise, he hadn't been hit.

Then he heard the reason why.

"Cage, you lunatic, get the hell out of there!"

Nook Kelly's voice.

Instantly, Clayton was suspicious. Was Kelly the hidden rifleman?

"Come up here, on the ridge," Kelly yelled. "Unless you've crapped your pants; then stay right where you're at."

Warily, Clayton stepped away from the cover of the shed, his Colt still in his hand. He saw Kelly on the rise, looking down at the misshapen bundle at his feet. Clayton walked closer and saw that the bundle was the body of a man.

When he was close enough to Kelly to speak without shouting, he said, "Who is it?"

He saw the lawman's quick, white grin.

"You should be honored, Cage. This here is, or was, Mr. Shack Mitchell, the highest-paid regulator and all-round bounty hunter in the business."

Clayton walked closer. "Did he speak? Did he say who hired him?"

"Hell no, he didn't speak. I put four rounds into him. I don't know who hired him, but I can tell you this, the services of ol' Shack didn't come cheap."

Clayton joined Kelly on the rise and looked at the dead man.

He was a gray-haired man, small, thin, somehow shrunken in death. He wore a black suit, threadbare, faded to a dark gray color, and a black plug hat. A Spencer rifle lay under his body and he had a belted Colt around his waist.

"He don't look like much," Clayton said.

"Maybe not, but Shack was something. If I hadn't happened along and heard the shooting, he would have killed you fer sure."

He looked hard at Clayton. "What the hell was that fool play, running like a rabbit from one place to another, all the time getting nearer to Shack's rifle?"

"My own rifle was on the horse. I needed to get a lot closer to use the Colt."

"He could've blown off your damn head, a grown man prancing around down there like a girl at her first barn dance."

Clayton felt a flush of cold anger but bit back the sharp retort he'd been about to make. Keeping his voice even, he said, "You said you happened along. Why did you do that, just happen along?"

"I talked to Moses Anderson in town. He said you were still here."

"So you came out after me."

"Yeah, I had a bad feeling about you being out here alone." Kelly grinned. "And I was right."

He frowned. "Hell, how long were you moping around in there?"

Clayton shook his head. "I don't know—minutes, I guess."

"More like hours."

"It could have been. I lost track of time."

"Shack was waiting for you to come out. He was a patient man."

"Seems like. Did you come up behind him?"

"Yeah. I saw him draw a bead on you and shot him in the back. Hell of a way to kill a man."

Kelly shrugged. "Pity, because I guess ol' Shack deserved better. But you were in trouble and I had to act."

Clayton smiled. "Nook, my troubles are just about to begin. And yours."

"What do you mean by that?"

"You'll see."

Kelly glanced at Clayton's feet. "What the hell is that?"

The kitten twined through Clayton's legs, rubbing herself against his boots.

"It's a kitten," Clayton said. Then, in a sudden burst of inspiration, "Her name is Miss Lee."

Chapter 58

Shack Mitchell's horse was tethered in a stand of wild oak behind the ridge.

Clayton threw a loop over the man's feet and dragged him to the front of the ranch house. Mitchell was small and light and he threw him over the saddle without any trouble.

"I'm going into the house for something," Clayton said. "Keep an eye on him."

"He ain't going anywhere," Kelly said.

"Here," Clayton said, picking up the kitten, "hold Miss Lee. I don't want her wandering away."

He walked to the house, then stopped and turned when he heard Kelly yell.

The kitten was struggling mightily to get out of the lawman's grasp.

"Hell," Kelly said, "it's like holding a roll of barbed wire."

He dropped the kitten and, after an outraged glance at the marshal, she followed Clayton into the house.

Clayton returned with a sheet of notepaper from Parker Southwell's desk and a yellow pencil. He held the paper against the door and wrote:

HE FALED.

Kelly looked over his shoulder. "What the hell does that mean?"

"It means Mitchell failed to kill me. What else would it mean?"

"There's an *I* in failed. *F-A-I-L-E-D*."

"Are you sure?"

"Yeah, I'm sure."

Clayton inserted the *I*, then showed the paper to Kelly.

HE FAiLED.

"Satisfied now?" he said.

Kelly nodded. "It's close enough. Now what are you going to do with it?"

"You'll see when we get back to town."

The marshal gave Clayton a lingering look. "I have a feeling that what you're planning doesn't bode well."

"For some folks it doesn't," Clayton said.

Bighorn Point was tinted with lilac light, the store windows rectangles of yellow, when Clayton and Kelly rode into town.

The dead man hanging over the horse attracted attention and a small crowd gathered, then followed the riders, eager for any diversion.

Clayton drew rein and turned to Kelly. "Maybe you don't want to see this."

The lawman smiled. "Look around you, Cage.

You're the only excitement in town. I guess I'll stick."

"You won't like it, Nook."

"Try me."

"Your funeral," Clayton said.

He rode to the bank and swung out of the saddle.

"Here," he said to Kelly, "hold Miss Lee."

Nursing scratches, the lawman said, "Just set her down. She won't run away."

"Suppose a big dog comes?"

"I'll shoot it."

Kelly watched, amused, as Clayton pinned his note to the back of Mitchell's shirt. Then he led the horse with its nodding burden onto the boardwalk in front of the building.

The double doors were large, ostentatious, their glass panels engraved with scenes from Greek mythology.

Clayton opened both wide, ignoring the outraged cries from the clerks inside. He led the horse to the entrance, slapped its rump, and sent it charging inside, Mitchell's body bouncing across the saddle like a rubber ball.

Turning on his heel, Clayton walked away, leaving chaos behind him. The frightened horse tried to bolt in every direction, its flying hooves upsetting desks, smashing furniture, overturning cabinets, putting the fear of God into everyone in the bank.

"Told you that you wouldn't like it," Clayton said as he walked past Kelly.

The marshal grinned. "Cage, you're under arrest. You and your cat."

"On what charge?"

"Don't worry. I'll come up with a few."

Chapter 59

"Marshal, I want that man charged with attempted murder, wanton destruction of property, and . . . and . . ."

Ben St. John's jowls quivered, his face black with anger.

"This is an outrage! My bank is wrecked and he"—a fat ringed finger stabbed in Clayton's direction—"is responsible."

"Mr. Clayton has agreed to pay all the damages," Kelly said.

Clayton, who had agreed to no such thing, ignored that and said, "Your paid killer failed." He looked at Kelly. "With an *I*."

"What the hell are you talking about?" St. John said.

For a moment the banker's eyes met Clayton's and he recoiled, like a man who's just stared into the sun.

He knows. Damn him, he knows.

Clayton reached into his pocket and threw five double eagles into St. John's face. "Mitchell didn't kill me. You can have your money back."

"Mitchell?" St. John said, kicking the fallen coins away from him. "Are you talking about the dead man you dumped in my place of business?"

"You should know," Clayton said. "You sent for him."

"I never saw that man before in my life."

St. John looked at Kelly, a pleading expression on his face. "Marshal, I'm one of this town's leading citizens. Are you just going to sit there and let me be abused in this way by a . . . saddle tramp?"

Kelly seemed to consider that; then he said, "Did you hire Shack Mitchell to kill Mr. Clayton?"

"Of course not. That's preposterous. Why would I want this man dead?"

"Because I know who you are," Clayton said.

Kelly was surprised. He'd expected St. John to fly into another rage, but the man said simply, "Who am I?"

Clayton rose to his feet, the hate in him as cold as ice. "Your real name is Lissome Terry. Do you remember a farm in Kansas and the farmer you shot and his wife, the high yeller woman you raped?"

Clayton felt Kelly's eyes burn on him.

"You're a raving lunatic," St. John said. "I've never been in Kansas."

"Yes, you have, Terry, you and Jesse and Frank

213

and them. The woman you raped was my mother, and after you'd done with her she hanged herself. You crippled my pa, and he's been in a wheelchair ever since."

St. John would not meet Clayton's accusing stare. *Oh God, those eyes, looking right into me. Lancing into me . . .* "Marshal Kelly, I want this man locked up. I want him charged and sent to Yuma for thirty years."

Kelly's voice was even, unhurried.

"Mr. St. John, I can charge him with leading a horse onto the boardwalk. That's a ten-dollar fine."

"The horse charged into my bank, with a dead man across the saddle."

"The horse got scared and bolted. It's still a ten-dollar fine."

"I'll speak to Mayor Quarrels about this. It's obvious that you and Clayton are in cahoots. Which one of you murdered the poor man you're trying to pass off as a hired assassin?"

"I did," Kelly said. "He was trying to kill Mr. Clayton."

"So you say."

"Right. So I say."

The marshal reached into his drawer and pulled out a stack of wanted dodgers. He thumbed through them until he found the one he wanted. He threw it across the desk to St. John.

"Shack Mitchell is wanted in the state of Texas for the murder of one James McFaul, a lawyer," he said. "Look at Mitchell's likeness. He's the man I killed today."

"The man you hired to kill me, Terry," Clayton said.

St. John shook his head. His quivering jowls and small bloodshot eyes gave him the look of an outraged hog.

"I'm in Bedlam," he said. "You're both raving mad."

"Don't leave town, Mr. St. John," Kelly said.

The man smiled. "I won't, Marshal. But you will. Depend on it."

Chapter 60

"Well, what do you think?" Clayton said after St. John left.

"About what?"

"Is he Lissome Terry?"

"I don't know."

"I do. He's Terry all right. I could feel the fear oozing out of him like sweat."

"That doesn't prove a thing. Get him in court and he won't sweat fear or anything else."

"He likes screwing black women," Clayton said.

Kelly smiled. "And what does that prove?"

"My mother was black."

"She was high yeller. You said so."

"She was black with a pink skin. Terry was a Southern boy. He knew what she was."

Kelly shook his head. "That's doesn't cut it, Cage."

"I was speaking to Moses Anderson at the ranch house. He says St. John is poking Minnie, the little gal who was Lee Southwell's black maid."

"So, he likes to screw black ladies. I can't hang him for that."

"Moses says whores have a habit of disappearing after St. John is finished with them."

Kelly smiled. "Cage, you keep calling him St. John. Does that mean you aren't sure yourself that he's Lissome Terry?"

"No, I'm sure all right. And I think Moses knows a lot more about the man than he's telling."

"Sometimes Moses is full of it, but I can talk to him."

"He knows everything that happens in Bighorn Point."

Kelly thought about that, then said, "I'll talk to him. And that black gal, what's her name?"

"Minnie." Clayton hesitated a moment, then said, "She's whoring, Moses says."

"Uh-huh."

"That doesn't surprise you?"

"Nothing blacks do surprises me."

Clayton felt that like a slap. He stroked the kitten on his lap. "You don't like colored folks much, do you, Nook?"

"Not much."

"And me?"

"What about you?"

"I'm part black."

Kelly looked at him. "Cage, I'll study real hard on that."

After a moment's hesitation, Clayton said, "Emma?"

"Yeah . . . *Emma.*"

Chapter 61

Ben St. John was seething. Mitchell had failed him. The moon would come up tonight and still shine on Cage Clayton.

One of the drunks who'd been hired by Moses Anderson told him he saw the black man blabbing to Clayton.

About what? How much did the man from Abilene know?

He hadn't had time to question Moses before he killed him, but still, the safest way had been to shut him up for good.

Thank goodness he lived a short ways out of town. St. John was able to tell his clerks that he was going out to walk off a headache. The .32 he'd used didn't make much of a bang, especially inside a rock-walled cabin.

Despite his vile mood, St. John smiled.

Moses and his woman had fed him collard greens, ham, and corn bread, washed down with buttermilk. He thanked them with—*Bang! Bang!*—a bullet to each of their heads.

But the greens had given St. John a slight case of indigestion, and now, when he burped, he tasted them all over again.

It had been a good meal, though, and the buttermilk had been nice and cold, served out of a clay jug.

"Are you all right, dear?"

His wife looked up from her embroidery, her long, horsy face concerned.

St. John lowered his newspaper. "I'm fine, dear. Perhaps a little touch of indigestion."

"Can I get you a seltzer?"

"No, I'll be just fine."

"I heard about the horse and the dead man," the woman said.

"Yes, that vandal Clayton did it. Drunk, of course. He should be locked up."

"He's the one who says he's in Bighorn Point to kill a man, isn't he?"

"Yes, more drunken talk. Just today I told Marshal Kelly to run him out of town."

"Can we save him?"

"No, my dear, he's beyond redemption."

"What a pity. But perhaps we could try by example to—"

"You know, I think I will have that seltzer," St. John said.

Damn, Edith was an irritating woman.

"Right away, dear."

He watched Edith's tall, bony body as she walked into the kitchen and felt no desire.

Sometime soon she'd have to go and he'd move in a woman more to his tastes. But not until this Clayton mess was settled.

Edith was in bed asleep. St. John shook his head at the scrawny wonder of her. Affection-wise, Ben St. John cared more for the Morgan mare he kept at the livery stable than he did his wife.

He reached into the bottom of the closet he reserved for himself and lifted out a dusty carpetbag, then returned to the parlor and sat at the table.

The blue Colt, its barrel expertly cut back to the length of the ejector rod, had lain in the bag for years, wrapped in an oil-soaked cloth. To St. John's relief, the revolver showed no signs of rust, and the mahogany handles glowed dull red in the firelight.

He cleaned and oiled the revolver, then loaded five chambers. The ammunition was a more recent acquisition, each .44-40 round made by a master craftsman in Fort Smith.

St. John balanced the Colt in his hand. He had killed three men with the gun, and Cage Clayton would be the fourth.

He nodded, his mind made up.

When you want a job done well, do it yourself.

Chapter 62

Cage Clayton answered the knock at his hotel room door with a gun in his hand and a scowl on his face.

Nook Kelly stood looking at him, his features just as grim as Clayton's.

"Come to collect my ten-dollar fine, Marshal?"

Kelly made no answer. He reached behind him, grabbed Minnie by the shoulder, and pushed her into the room.

"Tell Mr. Clayton what you told me, girl," he said.

Minnie looked terrified, her black eyes huge.

"Tell him, Minnie," Kelly said again. "He won't hurt you."

The girl's voice was a timid whisper. "Mr. Anderson is dead, and so is Miz Lucy."

"What happened?" Clayton said, a stirring of alarm in his belly.

"I don't know," Minnie said. "Miz Lucy, she tole me to visit for supper, but she didn't come to the door when I knocked. So I went inside and . . . and they was both lying dead."

Clayton looked over Minnie's head to Kelly. "St. John?"

"I don't know."

"Have you been to Moses's house?"

"Not yet. I thought you'd like to be there."

"Then let's go," Clayton said. He grabbed his hat, then looked at Minnie. "You go on home, girl. Nobody's going to harm you."

The girl sniffed. "I'm so scared, Mr. Clayton. Bad things is happenin' in this town. There's blood on the moon tonight, I seen it."

Clayton patted Minnie's shoulder. "You run straight home now. You'll be all right."

"Nobody in this town will be all right, not tonight, not any night," the girl said. "I'm frettin', Mr. Clayton, frettin' something awful."

Moses Anderson lived in a limestone cabin he'd built by himself, about a half mile north of town.

Clayton and Kelly walked in silence through a night lit by the blood moon. Around them dark arrowheads of pine stirred their branches in a gusting wind. The night was cool and smelled of rain and of the lightning that flashed soundlessly above the summits of the Sans Bois.

"Cabin's just ahead," Kelly said, breaking the quiet that had stretched between him and Clayton. "Yonder among the wild oaks."

Oil lamps still burned in the house, its windows rectangles of yellow light that splashed on the ground and tinted the leaves of the oaks.

From the outside, in the darkness, the cabin looked cheerful, welcoming, like an enchanted cottage in a fairy tale.

But inside, there was only blood and death.

· · ·

"Both shot in the head from close range," Kelly said. "The woman has powder burns on her forehead around the bullet hole."

"St. John shut them up," Clayton said. "He was worried about what else Moses could tell me."

"You don't know that," Kelly said, careful to not make it sound like an accusation.

"I know it. And so do you, but you won't admit it."

"I don't know who killed Moses Anderson and his woman," Kelly said. "You don't know either. And there it stands."

"Moses had hired hands out there at the Southwell Ranch," Clayton said. "One of them told St. John I was talking with him."

Kelly shook his head. "Cage, we don't know that's what happened. I can't arrest a man on unfounded suspicion."

"Then look around you, damn it, and try to solve this thing."

"Cage, I'm a cow town marshal, hired for my guns. I'm not one of them big city detectives who hunt for clues and solve crimes."

Clayton's eyes, blue as ice and just as cold, met Kelly's. "Then what happens, Marshal?"

"I don't know."

"Don't talk to St. John just yet. Ask his clerks if their boss left the bank for any reason yesterday. If they say he did, then you can talk to him and ask him where the hell he was."

"The people who work in St. John's bank won't tell me anything. They depend on him for their livelihood."

"You'll try?"

"Yes, Cage, I'll try."

Then Clayton said something that surprised Kelly and for a moment left him tongue-tied.

"Did you speak to Emma? About my mother?"

Clayton could see the lawman squirm, searching his reeling mind for words. Finally he said, "When I left her tonight, she was thinking about it."

"Not much to think about if you love a person."

Kelly made a strange face, almost a grimace. "She's thinking about any children you might have."

And right then Cage Clayton died a little death.

Chapter 63

"Mr. Clayton, you've played hob."

Mayor Quarrels mopped up the last of the gravy on his plate with a piece of bread and, to reinforce his statement, said, "Just . . . played . . . hob."

"Is that why you invited me to lunch, to tell me that?" Clayton said.

"Yes, that, and to ask you, nicely, mind, to get the hell out of my town."

Clayton smiled, but said nothing, waiting for the mayor to talk again.

They were the only customers in Mom's kitchen. Quarrels had made a late-afternoon appointment with Clayton for that very reason.

The mayor sat back in his chair, sighed, and lit a cigar.

"Since you got here, there's been nothing but death and destruction," he said. "Colonel Southwell, his wife, Shad Vestal, now Moses Anderson and his woman . . . the list seems to go on and on."

He stabbed his cigar in Clayton's direction. "To say nothing of the man you gunned in the saloon and the one you crippled."

Quarrels sighed and shook his head.

"I've got nothing against you personally, Mr. Clayton. You did well when you helped Marshal Kelly track down the Apaches, but, damn it all, you seem to have been born under a dark star."

The mayor attempted a smile, failed, then said, "You're a bad influence on this town and I want you far away from it."

Clayton waited while Mom refilled his coffee cup, then lit a cigarette and said, "I'll leave when I prove that Ben St. John is really Lissome Terry, the man responsible for the death of my mother."

"Nook Kelly told me about your suspicions. He says you also claim that Mr. St. John murdered Moses and his woman."

"He's right. I do, and I mean to prove it."

"All that is errant nonsense. Mr. St. John is a

valued member of this community, a man of impeccable reputation. Why would he commit murder, for heaven's sake?"

Clayton didn't feel like going into it. Nothing he could say would change Quarrels's mind anyway. He sat in silence, waiting. It was a while before the mayor spoke again.

Finally, as though he'd just gotten all his thoughts in order, Quarrels said, "Here's what we're willing to do—"

"Who's we?"

"Myself and the leading citizens of Bighorn Point."

"Ah."

"One thousand dollars in gold, Mr. Clayton, cash on the barrelhead."

Quarrels beamed. "What do you think of that?"

"What do you want in return?"

"Leave this town and never come back."

"Who's putting up the money? St. John?"

"He and others, including myself."

Clayton smiled. "Bighorn Point must want to get rid of me real bad. I must be a desperate character."

"Oh, we do and you are. I thought I made that clear."

What Clayton didn't want now was an ultimatum—*get out of town by dark or else.*

He played for time. "Let me study on it, Mayor. A thousand in gold is a lot of money."

Quarrels's face hardened. "All right, but don't think about it too long."

"I'll let you know my answer soon."

"For your sake, Mr. Clayton, I hope you decide to take the money."

Chapter 64

"Well, did your plan work? Did Clayton bite?"

Mayor Quarrels ushered Ben St. John into a chair in front of his desk.

When the fat man was settled, he said, "He's studying on it."

"I want him out of here, John, one way or another."

"I think he'll take the money and run."

"Damn it, I don't want 'I think.' I want 'I know.'"

"All right, then, Ben. I know he'll take the money."

St. John lit a cigar. "Back in the old days I would have taken care of this myself."

"Back in the old days you were good with a gun, Ben." Quarrels smiled. "You're a tad out of practice."

"I can still take him, if I have to."

"Maybe. Just remember to make it look good for Kelly."

Quarrels stepped to a tray of bottles and glasses in front of his office window. He poured three fingers of whiskey for himself and St. John and returned to his desk.

Without looking at the other man, Quarrels said, "Why Moses and his woman?"

St. John was startled and the hand holding his glass shook. "You know?"

Quarrels smiled. "Of course I know. I heard that Moses was seen talking to Clayton out at the Southwell Ranch. At first I didn't think much about it, but when Moses was shot, I started putting two and two together."

"I didn't want him talking to Clayton about the dead whores."

"Yeah, I figured that. I knew you were scared that Moses would blab to Clayton about the two ladies. After all, he helped you get rid of the bodies, remember?"

"He helped *us* get rid of the bodies."

"I owed you a favor, Ben, and I repaid it. Now, the way I look at it, you owe me one."

"And now you're calling it in."

"Under the circumstance, I consider it only right."

"All right, John, out with it. How much?"

Quarrels shrugged. "Talking money is so vulgar, but since this is between friends, let's call it two hundred a month."

St. John was aghast. "You mean, on top of what I already pay you?"

"Of course, Ben. Don't be a piker."

A hot scarlet anger gripped St. John, squeezing his chest, constricting his throat.

"I never liked you, Quarrels," he said, his voice tight. "I should've killed you back in Texas."

The mayor smiled. "I don't think so. I was faster than you, and so was Park. You came in a slow third, Ben."

St. John forced himself to calm down. "All right, another two hundred to keep your big mouth shut."

"Good for you, Ben. I mean, I'd hate to whisper in Edith's ear about the murdered whores. I reckon she'd walk out on you, Ben, and take her money with her." Quarrels grinned. "Now, that would be a real shame. Put you out of business, I should think."

He shook his head. "What a loss to the community."

"You've made your point. I'll pay you the money."

Quarrels rose and brought the whiskey bottle to the desk. He paused, the bottle in his hand, and raised his eyes to the ceiling.

"Ah, Ben, remember the good old days, you and me and Park? You recollect the banks we robbed, the folks we killed?"

He poured the whiskey into each of their glasses. "Remember the bank down Galveston way when you gunned that hick sheriff, then—"

"Shut your damned trap," St. John said.

"Gunned the sheriff, then went back that night and talked up his woman? 'Course, you was Lissome Terry back then. We called you Liss—at least I did. I can't recall what Park called you."

St. John rose to his feet. "Tell me if Clayton agrees to take the money. And from now on, let's keep our meetings to a bare minimum."

Quarrels grinned. "You don't like to talk about the old days, Ben, do you?"

St. John looked at the mayor, his eyes dead.

"You and me, our talking is done," he said. "For good."

For a long time, Mayor John Quarrels stared at the door that had slammed shut behind St. John.

He was a worried man. This Clayton business was getting out of hand.

Ben was starting to run scared and could do something foolish, like trying to shade Clayton on the draw-and-shoot.

Once Liss had been pretty good with a gun, but that had been a long time ago and even then he wasn't a named man, a feared gunfighter.

Clayton was no pushover. He could take Ben, Quarrels was sure of it.

And if that happened he'd lose his meal ticket.

The mayor's salary didn't run to Havana cigars and the best bonded bourbon he enjoyed. Or to high-class whores, for that matter.

Quarrels poured himself another drink.

Maybe he was worrying over nothing. There was always the chance that Clayton would take the thousand dollars and leave town.

As soon as the thought entered his head, he dismissed it.

Clayton wanted Ben dead and nothing else would satisfy him.

Quarrels held the cool glass to his hot forehead and closed his eyes.

Think, man. Think.

Then it came to him. . . .

Liss couldn't shade Clayton, but he could.

Back in the old days, Quarrels had been fast on the draw and had piled up enough dead men to prove it. Even as out of practice as he was, he was too good for Clayton. After all, what was the man? Nothing but a damned Kansas drover who'd gotten lucky against amateurs in the Windy Hall Saloon.

Quarrels drank, smiling around the rim of the glass.

Then it was settled.

He opened a drawer, pulled out a sheet of paper, and began to write.

After that was done, he carefully folded the paper, slipped it into an envelope, and scrawled *Cage Clayton* across the front.

He had one more letter to write, longer and more detailed. This he left on top of his desk where it would be easily found.

Quarrels's words to Clayton were written in ink, but he was confident they'd soon be branded across the man's consciousness in flaming letters a foot high.

He rose to his feet.

First have a boy deliver the envelope to Clayton's hotel, and then it would be time to call in another favor.

Chapter 65

"Kid brought this for you," the desk clerk said, stopping Clayton on his way out the door.

He handed over the envelope.

Clayton slipped out the folded paper, opened it up, and read.

The message was straightforward enough, but he scanned it twice to make sure his eyes were not playing tricks on him.

I can help you put a rope around Lissome Terry's neck.

Meet me at the Southwell Ranch at sundown.

There was no signature.

"Did the kid say who gave this to him?"

"No, he didn't," the clerk said. "Bad news?"

Clayton shook his head. "Good news, maybe."

Before the clerk could question him further, he

stepped onto the hotel porch and glanced at the sun.

There were still a couple of hours until dusk.

Clayton glanced over at the marshal's office, but there was no sign of Kelly, and that was good.

He planned to do this himself without Nook's meddling.

Clayton had no illusions about the note. The chances were high it was bait on a dangling hook designed to lure him into a trap.

He could be bucking a stacked deck, but he was willing to accept the odds.

St. John himself might have written the note, pushing for a showdown, as anxious as Clayton himself to get it over with.

He nodded to himself, his face grim.

Well, that suited him just fine.

But then another thought struck him—St. John was a careful and cunning man.

He wouldn't come alone.

Clayton walked to the livery and threw his saddle on Shack Mitchell's black.

Benny Hinton angrily stepped beside him. "Here, where are you taking that hoss?"

"Out."

"No, you ain't. The owner is deceased and his animal is now town property."

Clayton's nerves were stretched almost to the

breaking point and he was in no mood to suffer fools gladly.

Suddenly his gun was in his hand, the muzzle jammed between Hinton's shaggy eyebrows. "Are you going to give me trouble, old man?"

Hinton stepped back, scared, but still angry.

"You're bad news, Clayton. I knowed that the minute I set eyes on you. Take that hoss and I'll see ye hung fer it."

Clayton ignored the man and led the black from the stable.

Hinton followed him.

"After you steal the horse, why don't you keep on riding, Clayton?" he said. "Bighorn Point was a peaceful town until you got here."

"When I got here, old man, Bighorn Point was a cesspit and it still is."

He swung into the saddle and smiled at Hinton. "You take care now."

"And you go to hell."

Clayton stared down the dusty street, the shadows already stretching longer as the sky tinted red.

"Seems to me, hell is where I'm at," he said.

Chapter 66

As he rode through the deepening day, Clayton took the note from his shirt pocket and read it again, as though the letters would suddenly leap from the page and rearrange themselves into the name of the person who wrote it.

He knew with almost one hundred percent certainty that he was riding into a trap—but there was always a slim chance the note was genuine. To positively identify St. John as Lissome Terry was a gamble worth taking.

The sky above the Sans Bois peaks was rust red, streaked with pale lilac, when Clayton reached the Southwell Ranch.

When he was still a ways off, he drew rein and studied the house and the surrounding terrain to be sure he wasn't the target of a hidden rifleman.

Nothing moved and in the fading light the ranch house was silent, still, as though it had been abandoned a hundred years before.

But the house had a hold over him that Clayton did not understand.

It seemed that he was being constantly drawn to the place, a moth to flame, as though the dead were reaching out from the grave and beckoning to him.

Closer . . . Come closer. . . .

Clayton shifted in the saddle, uneasy. He felt he

was being watched by a thousand eyes, hostile, malevolent, cold.

His attention was drawn to the creek, where a solitary Hereford bull shambled to the water and drank. Suddenly the animal lifted his head and peered with shortsighted intensity toward the cattle pens.

After a full minute, the bull tossed his head and went back to drinking, apparently undisturbed by what he'd seen.

Clayton uneasily noted that.

It had probably been a prowling coyote or bobcat, neither of which would make the Hereford feel threatened.

But it could have been a man, a two-legged animal the bull had learned to trust.

Yet there was no movement around the cattle pens or the toolshed, and the Hereford finished his drink and walked away without another glance in that direction.

Clayton wiped his sweaty palms on his pants, then let the black pick its way forward.

He drew rein in front of the house, then stepped out of the leather to make himself a less conspicuous target.

The long summer daylight was lingering. Clayton glanced at the sun, sinking in the western sky like a copper penny. Maybe another hour until full dark.

To his right, the bunkhouse door was ajar,

creaking slowly on its hinges in a whisper of wind. Behind that, the barn, a smokehouse, and a corral, timber planks stacked up nearby for repairs that had never been done.

The place was deserted. Had the note been somebody's idea of a practical joke?

Feeling foolish, Clayton called out, "Anybody here?"

"Right behind you, Mr. Clayton."

Clayton felt the hair rise on the back of his neck. How could he have been blindsided like that?

He turned slowly, his hand away from his gun.

Then his jaw dropped when he saw the man standing there, smiling at him.

"Mayor Quarrels. How—"

The man smiled. "I could've gunned you. Easy. You must learn to take more care, Mr. Clayton. Of course, now it's too late."

His anger flaring, Clayton said, "Why are you here? Did you write the note?"

"Of course I wrote the note. I didn't tell a lie. I can put a rope around Lissome Terry's neck anytime I choose."

Quarrels stepped around Clayton and stopped when his back was facing the ranch house.

It was a seemingly casual move, but it set Clayton on edge, as did the style of the mayor's dress.

Gone was his businesslike broadcloth; in its place a black hat and shirt, black leather vest, pants of the same color, tucked into polished black boots. His gun belt was black; the only touch of color in his entire outfit the yellowed ivory handles of his Remingtons.

He looked, Clayton decided, like an outlaw from the cover of a dime magazine, but there was an aura of violence and danger about him, as palpable as the stench of an unwashed body.

"You sent me the note," Clayton said, painfully aware that he was restating what Quarrels had already told him.

"Yes," Quarrels said, smiling, offering him no help.

"About Lissome Terry."

"Yeah, him. I've already said all this."

"And you have information for me?"

Quarrels smiled. "Information? You know who Terry is. You don't need me to tell you."

"Ben St. John?"

"Huzzah for the man from Abilene."

"Were you there? I mean, in Kansas, when it happened?"

"I was there. I didn't see Liss screw the woman, but she squealed plenty, so we knew it was happening, me and Jesse and them."

"Why didn't you stop him?"

Quarrels shrugged. "Man wants to hump a woman, it's no concern of mine."

Keeping his anger in check, Clayton said, "Thank you for your help, Mayor. Now I can kill Terry with a clear conscience."

"Ah, but it's not as simple as that, Mr. Clayton."

"It is to me."

"Yes, I know. And that's why I'm going to kill you."

Chapter 67

Clayton was taken aback, but he tensed, ready.

He ran through names in his mind, gunfighters he'd heard men discuss: Wyatt Earp, John Wesley Hardin, Bill Longely, Harvey Logan, Dallas Stoudenmire, Ben Thompson . . . others.

But the name John Quarrels had never been mentioned that he could remember.

It didn't mean the man wasn't dangerous. He was. And he seemed supremely confident and that worried Clayton most of all.

Quarrels talked again.

"I need to keep St. John alive," he said. "I squeeze money out of the fat man"—Quarrels made a clenching motion with his fist—"until his eyes pop."

"You blackmail him by threatening to reveal his true identity."

Quarrels smiled. "Blackmail is such an ugly word. Let's just say Ben keeps me in a style to which I've become accustomed. That's why I can't allow you to gun him willy-nilly, as they say."

Quarrels glanced at the sky.

"Be dark soon, Mr. Clayton. Shall we get this unpleasantness over with?"

It was obvious to Clayton that Quarrels's talking was done, and he himself had no words left unsaid.

But after a struggle he managed to eke out a few that pleased him greatly.

"Quarrels," he said, "you're an even sorrier piece of trash than Terry."

The mayor of Bighorn Point smiled. And shucked iron.

Clayton took the hit on his feet, fired back. Whether he had scored or not, he had no idea.

Quarrels stood flat-footed, expertly getting in his work. Two more bullets hit Clayton.

He dropped to his knees, his head reeling, raised his Colt to eye level, and fired.

Hit hard, Quarrels staggered back a couple of steps.

Clayton fired again.

Another hit, somewhere low in the man's gut.

Quarrels backed up, bent over his gun. His back slammed against the house wall, and he straightened, ready to again take the fight to Clayton.

He ran his Remington dry, two shots kicking up dirt in front of Clayton's knees.

As Quarrels clawed for his other gun, Clayton got to his feet. Holding the Colt in both hands, he fired, fired again. He tried for a third shot, but the hammer clicked on the empty chamber.

But it was enough.

Through a shifting shroud of smoke, he saw Quarrels fall, and the man showed no inclination to get up again.

Clayton swayed on his feet. Blood was draining out of him and he figured his life along with it.

He ejected the Colt's empty shells and started to reload from his cartridge belt.

The bullet hit him like a sledgehammer.

He gasped in pain as the rifle round slammed into the left side of his waist near his spine. The .44-40 destroyed tissue on its way in, more as it exited his belly in an erupting fountain of blood and flesh.

Clayton fell on his back, struggling to stay conscious, blood in his mouth.

He thumbed off a shot in the general direction of the cattle pens.

It was a futile play born of desperation, but had the effect of driving the gunman out of hiding.

In the crowding gloom, Clayton had a fleeting impression of a tall, loose-limbed man with a drooping mustache running toward him, levering a Winchester from his shoulder.

Bullets kicked up around Clayton, one close enough to tug at the sleeve of his shirt. He laid the Colt on his raised knees, two-handed the handle, and got off a shot.

The rifleman stumbled, fell on his face. He tried to rise, but Clayton hit him again and this time the man's hat flew off. A killing head shot.

Slowly, Clayton eased himself on his back. He'd been hit multiple times and any one of them could be fatal.

He stared at the sky.

A star blazed above him, bright in a dark part of the night sky that slowly spilled ink over the last pale remnants of the blue bowl of the day.

The darkness gave birth to a wind that sighed around Clayton, tugging at him, teasing him, mocking his weakness. The black horse stepped close, its reins trailing. Seeing no reaction from its rider, it turned away and Clayton heard the receding *clop-clop* of its hooves.

He tried to rise, failed, lay down again.

Why was he feeling no pain? Was that a good thing?

No, it was bad. Maybe his spine was shattered.

He closed his eyes and listened into the rustling night.

Then a darker darkness than the night took him.

Chapter 68

Cage Clayton opened his eyes.

The moon was high in the sky and had modestly drawn a gauzy veil of cloud over its nakedness. He heard whispers, a woman's silvery laugh, the rustle of the wind.

He sat up, his eyes reaching into the night. They stood at the open door of the house, looking at him.

Suddenly Clayton was angry.

"Damn you both, you're dead!" he said.

Lee Southwell smiled at him. She wore a white dress, a scarlet heart in front where her breasts swelled.

"We've come for you, Cage," she said.

"Time to follow the buffalo, old fellow," Shad Vestal said.

"And I don't think I will. What do you think of that?" Clayton said.

He felt around him for his gun, his fingers flexing though the dirt.

"You're one of us now, Cage," Lee said. "You're one of the dead."

Vestal stepped out of the shadow of the door into the moonlight.

His head was a blackened dome of scorched flesh, bare, yellow bone showing, his eyes burned out.

"Parker Southwell is here, Cage," he said. "Join us now. We don't want to keep the colonel waiting."

"Damn you, Vestal," Clayton said. "You killed him."

"Yes, and now I suffer for it," Vestal said.

Lee stepped beside him, blood glistening on her breast.

"Would you like to sing, Cage?" she said. She looked at Vestal. "What shall we sing for Cage?"

She jumped up and down, then, gleefully, "Oh, I know. Listen, Cage. *In the sweet by and by, we shall meet on that beautiful shore.*"

"Shut the hell up!" Clayton yelled.

"In the sweet by and by, we shall meet on that beautiful shore."

Clayton's fingers closed on the handle of his gun. He fired at Lee, then Vestal.

After the racketing echoes of the shots were silenced by the night, Clayton staggered to his feet, a man so soaked in blood he looked like a manikin covered in red rubies.

"I done for you!" he cried out. "I done for you both! And be damned to ye!"

The moonlight splashed the front of the house with mother-of-pearl light, deepening the shadows. The still body of John Quarrels lay close to the front door.

Clayton sobbed deep in his chest and dropped to his knees.

"I . . . done . . . for . . . you," he said. "You came for me, and you rode my bullets back to hell."

And he fell on his face, and gladly he let the darkness claim him again.

Chapter 69

For the first time in years, Mayor John Quarrels was not at his desk at eight sharp, fresh as the morning itself and eager to meet the challenges of the day.

Or so his clerk thought.

To a mousy little man like Clement Agnew, the mayor's office was a hallowed spot, not to be intruded upon unless the business was urgent.

Agnew tapped on the door again. No answer. He rapped harder, with the same result.

Swallowing hard, he threw open the door and stepped inside.

From the doorway Agnew noticed a paper on the blotter. Perhaps it was a note of explanation for His Honor's absence.

But dare he read it? Perhaps it was official town business and strictly confidential.

The clerk hesitated, then made his decision.

The mayor was missing, so this was an emergency.

Agnew rounded the desk and picked up the paper. As a summer rain rattled on the windows, he read and grew pale. Then, as though demons were chasing him, he ran out of the office and didn't stop running until he reached the marshal's office.

Nook Kelly listened to the clerk's concerns about Quarrels and his horror and disbelief when he read what the mayor, a respected and much loved man, had written.

The marshal calmed Agnew and sent him on his way with the assurance that "All will be well."

Then he read the note.

Marshal Kelly,

I'm sure you will be among the first ones to read this, and when you do I will already be dead.

There were three of us came up the trail from Texas: Colonel Parker Southwell, Lissome Terry, and me. We came with a stolen herd and a considerable amount of money, notes and gold coin, the spoils from the banks, trains, and stagecoaches we'd been robbing for years.

Just before we rode up on Bighorn Point, Park said me and Terry should use new names, since we were wanted men in Texas. The colonel, on account of him being the brains of the outfit, never took part in the robberies and was unknown to the Rangers. Besides, he had honorably worn the gray and was above suspicion.

I became John Quarrels and Terry took the name Ben St. John. He said it had a ring to it.

Later I became mayor and Ben and Park prospered.

I was with Ben, though back then I called him Liss, when he shot the farmer up in Kansas and done his wife, though I took no part in either the shooting or the rape.

Down in Texas he killed a lawman and went back that same night and raped his grieving young widow. Park just smiled and said Liss was "a scamp, and no mistake."

But Liss shouldn't have done them rapes and killings, because I blackmailed him with them and he became my "meal ticket."

But now I am dead, and I don't give a damn. Liss should get what he deserves—a rope around his neck.

I'm meeting Cage Clayton at the Southwell Ranch this evening. I can't let him kill Liss and dry up my source of money. But if Clayton is faster on the draw than me, you will read this note. Just be aware that I regret nothing.

Yours Respct.
John Quarrels, Esq.

Kelly dropped the note on his desk, then stepped to the window, rain running down the panes like a widow's tears.

Clayton had been right all along. Ben St. John was Lissome Terry, the man responsible for his mother's death.

Was Cage still alive?

The fact that he'd read the note suggested he was. But he could be wounded, unable to move.

Kelly shrugged into his slicker, put on his hat, and picked up Quarrels's letter.

It was time to talk to St. John.

He shook his head, angry at himself.

No, it was time to talk with Lissome Terry.

The door opened and Emma Kelly stepped inside. She pushed back the hood of her rain cape and smiled at Kelly. "Well, are you treating me to breakfast?"

"Not today, Emma," he said.

He gave her the note and waited until she read it.

"I think Cage is still at the Southwell place and he might be wounded," Kelly said.

The girl was confused, overwhelmed by the ramifications of Quarrels's words. "What are you going to do?" she said.

"Arrest St. John, or Terry, then go look for Cage."

"He could be dead by then."

"The way I see it, my duty to this town must come first."

"But Cage is your friend."

"Emma, he'd want me to jail Terry before anything else."

"Then I'm riding out there. You can follow when St. John—Terry—whatever he's called—is behind bars."

Kelly smiled. "You love Cage Clayton, don't you?"

Emma nodded, but said nothing.

"All right, go after him. We're wasting time talking here."

"Nook, just one thing." The girl hesitated, then said, "How black is Cage?"

The question surprised Kelly, but he answered it.

"I don't know. A tenth? A twelfth? Only his mother could've told him for sure, and even then she might not have known herself."

He looked at Emma, her face dewy fresh from the rain, her eyes clear blue. "Does it really trouble you that much? Cage looks as white as me, or you, come to that."

"There's a . . . consideration involved, Nook. But I don't want to talk about it right now."

"Then we'll discuss it later."

Kelly opened the door and he and Emma stepped into the slanting rain.

"I'll see you at the Southwell place," he said. "And let's pray to God that we're not too late."

Chapter 70

Kelly, rain dripping from his hat and slicker, stormed into the bank, letting a glass door slam shut behind him.

A startled clerk looked up from the counter, his face registering puzzlement, then shock.

"Where's St. John?" the marshal said.

The clerk fumbled for words, finally found his tongue, and said, "He's with a client and can't be disturbed."

Kelly walked to the end of the counter, lifted the flap, and strode purposely toward St. John's door. He tried the handle but the door was locked.

He looked at the clerk. "You, key!"

The man wrung his hands, his face anguished. "Marshal, there's only one key to that door and Mr. St. John locked it from the inside."

He managed a weak smile. "If you'd care to wait . . ."

Kelly smiled in turn, nodded. Then raised his boot and smashed the door in, splintered oak erupting from the lock. The door slammed hard against the wall and Kelly heard the terrified clerk shriek.

St. John, his huge arm draped over Minnie's narrow shoulders, jerked his head toward the door. Now he hurled himself up from the leather couch.

"This is an outrage!" the man yelled, his face purple with fury.

Minnie leaped from the couch.

"Marshal Kelly, I didn't do nothing," she said. "I'm a good girl. Honest, I am."

"Get out of here, Minnie," Kelly said.

The girl hurriedly stepped toward the door, then stood as still as a statue, her eyes wide as silver dollars, as Kelly said, "Wait!"

He looked at St. John. "Pay her."

"What?"

"I said, pay her."

The fat man protested. "Damn you, I never even started."

Suddenly a Bulldog was in Kelly's hand. "Pay her or I'll put one right in your fat gut."

St. John tried to retreat into bluster. "Kelly, I'll have your job for this. I'll see you jailed."

Kelly thumbed back the hammer of the Bulldog, shortening the trigger pull so much a breath of wind could set it off.

"I won't say it again, Terry. Pay her."

The fat man blanched and his jowls trembled. "That's not my name."

Kelly pushed the Bulldog forward and St. John immediately reached into his pocket and found a coin.

"Double, Terry. Pay her double."

"Marshal Kelly, you don't need to—"

"Shut up, Minnie."

St. John, badly frightened, dropped money into the girl's hand.

"Now get out of here, Minnie," Kelly said.

The girl fled and Kelly motioned with the gun. "Sit at the desk, Terry."

The fat man did as he was told, his slack mouth twitching.

A moment later the clerk stuck his head in the doorway.

"Are you all right, Mr. St. John?"

Kelly turned on him, his gun up and ready. "Get the hell away from here."

The clerk squealed and scampered back from the door. Kelly pushed it shut behind him.

He stepped to the desk and threw the paper in front of the fat man.

"Read it," he said.

St. John glanced at the note. Immediately his eyes popped and his hands trembled. He looked up at Kelly. "What are you showing me? The mayor is dead?"

"Read it," Kelly said.

The fat man's eyes dropped to the paper. When he finished reading he looked like a man about to have a heart attack.

"Lies," he said, his voice a whisper. "It's all lies. I have lawyers. I can beat this."

"I'll let the United States Marshal decide that, Terry. And I'll wire the Texas Rangers. I'm sure they'll be interested."

St. John raised bloodshot eyes to Kelly's face, the threat of the Rangers scaring him badly. "What will happen to me?"

"I'll hang you. Or the Rangers will."

St. John sat in silence for a while, then said, "Do I have an out?"

"Not that I can see," Kelly said.

"Money?"

Kelly shook his head.

"I should have gunned Quarrels years ago," the fat man said. "When he first began to squeeze me."

"Seems like."

St. John's hand strayed to the bottom drawer of his desk.

"Open it, Terry," Kelly said, his eyes glittering. "Please."

The fat man pulled his hand away as though it had been burned.

"On your feet," Kelly said.

"Where are you taking me?"

"To jail. Where you belong."

Chapter 71

There was no letup in the rain as Emma Kelly rode into the Southwell Ranch.

Lightning hissed across a sullen sky, and thunder rolled with the racketing din of a thousand strident drums.

She saw the bodies of three men sprawled on the

muddy ground. Clayton she recognized at once, lying on his back, his face turned to the rain.

Emma stepped from the saddle and ran to Clayton. Heedless of the mud, she kneeled, then lifted his head and laid it on her lap.

"Cage, can you hear me?"

The man's face, pale under his tanned skin, showed no sign of life.

Emma's hand moved to his bloody chest. His heart was still beating, but hesitantly.

Desperately the girl looked around her, her eyes searching for help that wasn't there. She saw only the shifting curtain of the rain, heard it chatter on the ranch house roof, smelled the caustic tang of lightning.

There was no one else. She had it to do.

Clayton was a big man, heavy with bone and muscle, and lifting him was out of the question.

Emma stood, grabbed him by the armpits, and dragged his limp body.

It was slow going, a few inches at a time, the man a heavy burden for a slender woman.

Starting and stopping, Emma took almost ten minutes to drag Clayton the twenty yards to the house. She glanced at Quarrels's body, curled up in death, and felt only anger.

She opened the door, and with the last of her strength, pulled Clayton inside into the hallway.

This was not the time for false modesty. Now, out of the rain, Emma stripped off Clayton's wet clothes and left him lying naked for a few moments while she ran into a bedroom and returned with a pillow and blanket.

The man was shot through and through, but he was still breathing, and that gave the girl hope.

Cage was strong. He would survive this—he had to.

She walked to the door and looked out into the raging morning.

She badly needed Nook Kelly's help, his man's strength.

When would he get here?

To the north of the Southwell Ranch, across the rain-lashed hill country, Marshal Nook Kelly stood in the bank and listened to Lissome Terry's proposition.

"Let me go to your office by myself, Nook," the fat man pleaded. "I don't want to walk through town with my hands raised and a gun at my back. I have friends here, neighbors."

Kelly glanced into the street. It was deserted, the rain forcing everyone indoors.

"There's nobody on the street, Terry," he said. "Now move your fat ass off the chair."

"For old times' sake, Nook?"

"Terry, you and me don't have old times, only bad times. Now move it. I won't tell you again."

Years ago, when Bighorn Point was wilder and Kelly more on edge, he'd trained himself to expect the unexpected, to be ready for something he'd never seen before.

That morning in Terry's office he wasn't unready—but his edge had been dulled by too many years of easy living.

And the fat man showed him something.

As he raised himself from his chair, he groaned, then slumped to his right, as though suddenly taken ill.

Kelly holstered his gun and started to step around the desk to help Terry to his feet. But the man suddenly straightened and stood up. It was very fast for a grossly overweight man, and Kelly was taken by surprise.

He drew as Terry's Colt came up, but the fat man surprised him again.

Instead of turning his gun on Kelly, Terry shoved the muzzle against his temple and pulled the trigger.

The Colt roared and blood and brains splattered the marshal's face.

"You killed him!"

The bank clerk ran inside and cast a horrified look at Terry's body. The fat man lay facedown on his desk, a pool of blood spreading around his head.

"He killed himself," Kelly said. "Damned coward couldn't stand proud and take his medicine like a man."

"Hell, what did he do?" the clerk said.

"Everything," Kelly said. "Everything that's bad."

Chapter 72

Cage Clayton watched the hazy play of light and shadow on the wall as he regained consciousness one hazy memory at a time.

The gunfight with John Quarrels and his bushwhacking buddy . . . the bullets thudding into his body . . . Lee Southwell and Shad Vestal mocking him from the shadows . . .

Ghosts of his imagination they'd been, those two, with as little substance as the filmy memories that now came and went in his head.

He raised himself up off the pillow, a movement that hurt him badly and one he did not care to repeat.

Where the hell was he?

From outside he heard a hammer clang on an anvil. Closer, a woman's voice, singing a song he didn't know.

Emma's voice.

Then a sound he recognized, the slow *tock* . . . *tock* . . . *tock* of the grandfather clock in the hallway of the Southwell ranch house.

Steeling himself for the pain he knew would result, Clayton propped himself up on an elbow.

"Emma!"

The girl responded immediately. She walked into the room, her smile as bright as a spring morning.

"My patient is finally awake," she said. "It's about time."

"And he's hungry," Clayton said.

Emma sat on the bed. "And that doesn't surprise me."

"How long . . ."

"Three weeks. You've been out of your head most of the time."

The girl made a face. "And who, may I ask, is Dallas Laurent?"

"Huh?"

"Dallas Laurent. You talked about her quite a bit, made me blush at times."

Clayton looked like a shy schoolboy. "Oh yeah, she was a woman I knew in Abilene."

"Was she pretty?"

"Yeah, I guess so. Last I heard she was in Denver, opened her own house."

"Now a lot of what you were saying makes sense." Emma sniffed.

Clayton was spared a further female interrogation when Nook Kelly stepped into the room. It was the first time he'd seen him without his guns.

"How are you doing, old fellow?" Kelly said.

"Peachy. Apart from carrying a ton of lead inside me."

Kelly laid a reassuring hand on Clayton's shoulder. "No, the doc got it all out, saved your life. Well, him and Emma. She hasn't left your side in weeks, and you raving like a madman, jumping in and out of death's door."

"Raving about Dallas Laurent?"

"Yeah, her, and less important stuff like cows and grass and winter snows."

Emma rose to her feet. "I'll fix you something to eat, Cage. Any preference?"

"How about burning me a huge steak with six fried eggs, a loaf of sourdough bread, and a gallon of coffee?"

The girl smiled. "Two soft-boiled eggs and a piece of toast, it is." She looked at Clayton. "I'll see what I can do about the coffee."

"Emma knows best, Cage," Kelly said, grinning. "That's something you'll learn."

After the girl was gone, Clayton said, "And Lissome Terry? Did I rave about him?"

"He's dead, Cage."

Kelly answered the question he saw on Clayton's face.

"He shot himself."

"But when? I mean, how—"

Using as few words as possible in the face of Clayton's growing impatience, Kelly told him about Quarrels's letter and the confrontation in the fat man's office.

"Terry couldn't take his medicine," he said. "I don't know what scared him worse, me or the Rangers. I guess he realized them boys would've taken him back to Texas and hung him for sure."

Clayton lay back on his pillow, his face a tangle of conflicting emotions. "Then it's over."

"Yes, it's over, and Bighorn Point will never be the same again."

Smiling, Kelly shook his head. "You played hob, Cage."

The marshal stepped to the door, then turned. "I'm shoeing the black for you. Feels good to work with my hands."

Clayton said nothing.

"Cage, it's over and now your life is just beginning," Kelly said. "Marry Emma and be happy and forget you ever heard the name Lissome Terry."

Chapter 73

After Clayton ate what Emma described as "an invalid's meal," she helped him sit up on the pillows.

"I've never been one to lie in bed," he said. "Hell, Nook is even shoeing my horse."

"You'll be very weak for a while yet," the girl said. "Dr. McCann said you can get up and start walking around in another couple of weeks."

Clayton shook his head. "Not here. Not in this house. Help me on my horse and I'll head back to the hotel."

Emma managed a lopsided smile. "Cage, you're not exactly welcome in Bighorn Point. You robbed them of their mayor and the proprietor of

259

the town's only bank. St. John's—I mean, Terry's—wife already packed up and left. She didn't leave a forwarding address."

"Robbed is not the word I'd have used," Clayton said.

"I know, but that's how the good citizens see it."

Emma, as though a thought had just occurred to her, held up a hand to stop Clayton from saying anything. She stepped into the silence. "You don't like this house?"

"No, it's a death house, a bad luck house. You bring sunshine to the place, but its darkness remains."

"But what about your job? Where will we live?"

"I don't want the job. We'll go back to Abilene. The cabin on my ranch is nothing like this place, but we can make it work."

Emma said, "Cage, when I'm your wife I'll go with you anywhere—you know that—and I'm willing to marry you today if you want."

"I can see a 'but' in your eyes."

"We have a problem."

"It's nothing we can't solve together, Emma, you and me."

"You're right. We can solve it, but it will take a sacrifice on both our parts."

"I'm willing to sacrifice. Just tell me what I have to do."

"I talked to Doc McCann when he was here, and he . . . Well, he confirmed my worst fears."

Clayton was genuinely puzzled. "What fears?"

"Cage, we can never have children."

"You don't want children?"

"Oh, I do, but that will be impossible."

Clayton shook his head. "Now you have me really confused."

Emma sat in silence for long moments, marshaling her thoughts; then, word by word, she began to break Cage Clayton's heart.

"Cage, you're part black. I know it's a very small part, but it's there."

Wary now, Clayton tried to make light of it. He said, "Maybe it's one of my toes—the black part, I mean."

"It's not. It's inside you somewhere, in your blood."

Before Clayton could say anything, the words wrenched out of Emma, as though every syllable caused her pain.

"Cage, we could have . . . a *throwback*."

Too stunned to say anything, Clayton could only stare at her.

The girl covered her face with her hands and said between sobs, "Listen to me, Cage. Try to understand. How would it look to other people to see me, a white woman, nursing a . . . a . . ."

"I understand," Clayton said after a long while. "I understand perfectly how you feel. You were raised with a certain attitude and it's hard for anyone to drop the prejudices of a lifetime."

Emma let her hands fall to her sides. "We can still marry, Cage. I'll make you happy. I'll be a good wife to you, I swear I will."

Clayton shook his head. "I want children someday, Emma. White, black, half-and-half, I don't care. I'll still love them."

Her pain giving way to defiance, Emma said, "I can't do that."

"I know you can't, Emma," Clayton said. "And I pity you."

Three hours later, wearing clothes he didn't originally own, Cage Clayton climbed onto the black.

He was very weak, his heart so shattered he thought it would never mend.

Kelly hung a sack of supplies on the saddle horn and passed Clayton Miss Lee.

"Cage, I'm sorry," he said.

"We're all sorry, Nook."

"Ride easy, pardner, and get better, huh?"

"Sure thing."

"Write. Let us know that you and your cat got back to Abilene safely."

"Yeah, I'll do that."

Cage Clayton turned his horse north, heading for home, a place where he could heal his body, and his soul.

He did not look back.

Epilogue

Cage Clayton returned to Kansas, where he reconciled with his father and prospered in the cattle business. He is credited with introducing Brahman cattle to the Kansas range.

He married in 1896 and had a large brood of towheaded kids.

Clayton died of influenza in 1930 at the age of eighty.

Nook Kelly died in 1906 while working as a laborer on the construction of the Panama Canal.

Emma Kelly married a preacher, then moved to Oklahoma City. Thereafter she disappeared from the pages of history.

The railroad never reached Bighorn Point and during the automobile age the main highways bypassed the town. By 1928 Bighorn Point was a ghost town and today only the limestone foundations of the church remain, almost invisible in the prairie grass.

The Southwell Ranch never prospered, and in 1918 the land was sold to the Standard Oil Company.

Angus McLean returned only once to Bighorn Point, to erect a headstone over Moses Anderson's grave that has since disappeared.

At least, that's how the story goes. . . .

Center Point Large Print
600 Brooks Road / PO Box 1
Thorndike ME 04986-0001 USA

(207) 568-3717

US & Canada:
1 800 929-9108
www.centerpointlargeprint.com